WHISPER FALLS
THE TOWN THAT DREADED HALLOWEEN
STEVE BERNARDI

Also By Steve Bernardi

The Bonesbury Chronicles

Book 1 - How to Succeed in Skeleton Business

Whisper Falls

The Town That Dreaded Halloween

Cover Illustration by Tina Olah

Full-Page Interior Illustration by Val Love

1st edition 2025
ISBN: 978-1-0693674-0-2

This book is dedicated to Stephen King, John Carpenter, Ray Bradbury, Michael Dougherty, and R.L. Stine, the true gods of Halloween.

Contents

Halloween Surprise

"Invention, my dear friends, is 93% Perspiration, 6% Electricity, 4% Evaporation, and 2% Butterscotch Ripple." -Willy Wonka (Gene Wilder), 1971

2~

To the average depressed adolescent, Jeremy Gaunt looked like he had it made. He was relatively healthy, had two parents who loved him, and got decent grades in school without really trying. To a moderately well-adjusted teenager, though, he might appear a bit sad. No matter what Jeremy did, the kids in his class never seemed to understand him or be on his side. And those same loving parents worked jobs with long hours that left little time for their son, pulling in revenue that left room for little but the bare necessities.

In Jeremy's younger days, there were two hours between the end of school and the end of his mother's shift at work. Sitting at home alone was no fun, so every day he would march himself down to Scott's Grocery to pester his mother with questions like what was for dinner, or if she could help him with question four of his math homework. Not wanting to lose her patience, Mrs. Gaunt would lovingly send Jeremy next door to the toy store to occupy himself. This was fine for a while, but coveting toys and games that your family could never afford was a hobby with diminishing returns.

No, young Jeremy would have to get creative if he wanted something interesting to do. He wouldn't have to go far, as three doors down from Montani's Toys, nestled between a laundromat and a place for buying car insurance, was a shop that had always drawn Jeremy's eye. 'Odd Curiosities' read a pine green sign over the front window. The letters may have at one point been gold or pearl inlay, but now they were a dull brown which was hard to read, and cracks ran at odd angles along the surface of the board.

There was no entertainment value in perusing things you wanted, Jeremy had learned. To an optimistic nine-year-old mind, looking at boring old antiques and books for fun made a strange kind of sense. Jeremy pressed his face against the glass to look inside, but they were tinted dark green like a wine bottle and impossible to see through.

When he opened the door, a pleasant bell chimed. In truth, it was like a hundred other bells that Jeremy had heard thousands of times in countless other stores and businesses, but something about this one was more inviting than the others. When he stepped through the threshold, his nose was overwhelmed by a musty odor. It called to mind a life long-lived, the scent of a building filled to the brim with knickknacks and other old wonders. Jeremy felt a bit like he was in his grandmother's house.

Behind the front desk, which was made of glass and contained four shelves of rings and other tiny objects, sat a man reading a book. If he had noticed Jeremy come in, he gave no indication of it, and that was fine by Jeremy, since strangers made him nervous. There were two identical mahogany shelving units behind the man which contained all manner of items. There was a teddy bear which could have been old enough to belong to Jeremy's grandparents slumped lazily on the highest shelf. A cubby on the bottom right was filled to the brim with scrolls of brittle paper. What drew Jeremy's eye the most was a human skull with an aquamarine gem embedded in its forehead, far out of reach on the top left.

The rest of the shop was immediately jarring to look at, with every angle seeming to change its dimensions. Every high corner was filled with large, round mirrors like the kind found in supermarkets, which Jeremy's mother had told him were to discourage theft. Because the shop was smaller than a supermarket, though, they gave a false sense of space, which bewildered the mind horribly. The front desk was directly ahead of the doorway, and the bulk of the shop was off to the side. Freestanding shelves with items on either side created a series of aisles, and other items cluttered the surrounding walls or hung on hooks. When Jeremy stepped past the front desk, his vision shifted again, and three shelves became seven. After convincing himself they were always like that, he began to peruse.

On one shelf sat a red orb with an uneven checkered pattern on it. Like the rest of the shop, the inner facets seemed to move as the observer moved, creating an effect akin to dozens of squares and rectangles crawling inside like insects. Further down was a boardgame made from carved wood, with strange beasts Jeremy didn't recognize on the surface of the box. It reminded him of their family's many game nights, but something told him this was in a different league than Monopoly.

When Jeremy reached the end of the first aisle, he saw the most beautiful display. In one of the corners he couldn't see from the front hung a forest of crystal balls, some held by string and others by chain, all different sizes and colors, no two being the same distance from the ground. A gentle breeze from when he had come in made them sway ever so slightly, the light caught in them bouncing and refracting dozens of times. There was just enough space in between them all for a person to stand, and Jeremy felt compelled to be there. As he got closer, he thought he could hear the orbs whispering, some directly to him and others chattering on to no one in particular.

"I wouldn't do that if I were you," called an even voice from across the room. Jeremy spun around, his heart suddenly racing as if he had been caught doing something improper. The shopkeeper had put his book down and was staring at Jeremy with thinly veiled annoyance. "I said I wouldn't go in there if I were you; likely to break something."

"You mean the crystal balls?" Jeremy asked innocently.

"Yes, those too. Now, if we're going to converse you may as well come here; I detest shouting, especially in my shop."

Jeremy did as he was told. Many more things caught his focus on the way back to the front, but something about the way the man had told him to come had made Jeremy feel he shouldn't delay. The shopkeeper got off of his stool and looked down at Jeremy with quiet appraisal.

"I'm sorry for yelling, mister..."

"Edwin Murd," said Edwin Murd.

"Okay, Mister Murd. I'm Jeremy, Jeremy Gaunt."

"I didn't ask." The insult went unnoticed by Jeremy, who eyed the items in the counter as if he were at an arcade with a handful of tickets.

"Where did you get all these things, Mister Murd?"

"Oh, lots of places. I've travelled a fair bit, and I tend to pick up things along the way. Some things people sell to me, or trade if I have something they believe they require. Very rarely I'll make something myself and put it on display."

"And people really want to buy this stuff?"

"Not usually, no," said Murd with a smug grin on his face. "But I am an excellent salesman."

Jeremy approached the counter and leaned on it, doing his best to imitate a tough cowboy he'd seen in one of his dad's favorite westerns. "How good are you?"

The shopkeeper narrowed his eyes, lamenting the smudges that would now be on his nice clean workstation. "I can sell anything to anybody."

"Prove it."

"Alright," Murd said, a playful smile creeping through his prickly veneer. "As you're the only customer currently in the store, you'll be my mark."

"What's a mark?"

"Oh," he smirked. "It just means someone who is about to be sold something. So tell me, Jeremy Gaunt, what is it you desire?"

Jeremy thought hard as to how he would answer this question. Even at a young age, he understood that a majority of his family's problems, and by extension his own, could be solved by having more money. But asking for more money would be silly, like asking a genie for more wishes; it just wasn't allowed.

"Do you have anything that could make me more popular at school?"

"Aah," Murd chirped. "Acclaim, favor, recognition. A pitiful thing like you, likely friendless and at the mercy of bullies most days, yes?"

"Not really." Jeremy was starting to pick up on the cutting undertones of Mister Murd's dialogue, but he chose to ignore it. Sticks and stones, his mother would say. "I have lots of friends, and bullying isn't allowed at school."

"How dreadfully modern."

"But it would be cool to be really popular. We had a magician perform for us last year, and everyone liked her a lot. Do you have anything like a magic kit?"

"Ha!" shrieked the shop owner. "Stepped into the unknown not ten minutes ago, and already he wants to dabble in the arcane. I'll tell you a secret, boy, and we'll call it a freebie, at that: magicians are pompous, self-important buffoons. You would do well in life to avoid them at all costs. No, I will not sell you a 'magic kit'; both of us can do better."

Mister Murd turned his back and began sorting through items on the shelves behind him. Now that he had the opportunity to get a good look, Jeremy could see just how densely packed they really were.

There was a jade mask whose face was half smile and half frown, which was positioned in such a way that it seemed to stare down at Jeremy. Below it there was a knight's gauntlet, its steel colored in a gold and blue flourish. There were also numerous unmarked boxes and other containers, arranged in no discernible order, and these seemed to be the focus of Murd's search.

"Aha!" he cheered triumphantly. Jeremy blinked, and he could have sworn he saw Murd's entire arm disappear as it reached back into the conflictingly shallow cubby. He rubbed his eyes, and when his vision cleared, Murd had retrieved a hickory-colored box which was a perfect cube, save for a set of hinges on one side.

"I guarantee this will make you the most popular boy in your school." Murd opened the box in front of Jeremy's face. Cushioned in gold velvet lining was a beautiful red yo-yo. Its surface was made out of material Jeremy didn't recognize, but it was smoother and more perfectly red than any toy that had ever graced the aisles of Montani's. Adorning the front face was an azure blue star made out of some sort of crystal, or perhaps merely convincing plastic.

"I have to have it," said a transfixed Jeremy, his eyes never leaving the box once. "How much?"

"How much money do you have on you?" Murd raised an eyebrow.

"I... I don't have any." He tried to hide it, but saying that out loud actually made Jeremy a little sad.

"Well," scoffed Murd, closing the box with a swift mechanical motion before placing it back on the shelf. "How am I to prove my remarkable skills as a salesman if my mark is without coin?"

"I guess you can't," Jeremy muttered. "Can I come back tomorrow?"

"Will you be bringing money?"

The boy pondered for a minute. "I don't think so?"

"Then I honestly don't care what you do."

Jeremy murmured a hasty goodbye and skipped out of the store. The experience had left him feeling oddly positive, even though he acknowledged on the surface that Mister Murd had said some mean things. Every once in a while, a kid at school would be mean, and Jeremy's parents told him that mean kids were usually just hurting inside, or trying to feel better about themselves. Being mean back never solved anything, so it was best to turn the other cheek instead, whatever that meant. Jeremy concluded that Mister Murd could use a friend.

That night at dinner, Jeremy's parents asked him a series of questions concerning things like how his day was and what he had learned in school. He answered them all with mild interest and complete honesty, which was standard operating procedure during meals in the Gaunt household.

"See anything cool in the toy store?" Alan Gaunt asked his son.

Jeremy couldn't say why he was about to lie to his father. Perhaps he didn't feel like explaining why he had chosen a musty junk store over a den of toys and merriment. Maybe he didn't want his parents to think ill of Mister Murd before meeting him, or worse, tell Jeremy he couldn't go back. It was possible that Jeremy just liked the idea of having a secret from his parents, a benign one, shared only between himself and Mister Murd. Whatever the reason, Jeremy quickly thought up an untruth which would appeal to his father's sensibilities.

"They got new chess sets in."

"Aah!" said Alan, nodding emphatically with a warm smile. "You know what I always say about chess."

"It's a man's game."

"That's right! A battle of wits, cerebral might versus intellectual cunning. You can't get that from video games."

"They make chess video games, dear," teased Kelly Gaunt, who was utterly smitten with the ridiculous man she had married.

"They do?" Alan made an exaggerated face of puzzlement, which never failed to make Kelly and Jeremy laugh.

"Can I go to my room?" Jeremy asked politely. "I have some homework to finish."

"Sure thing, sweetie," said his mother.

This was another calculated deception. Jeremy had returned home earlier than normal after leaving Curious Oddities, and so he had done his homework then. In reality, Jeremy was just tired. The remainder of the evening was spent reading, during which Jeremy sketched countless yo-yos in the margins of his books.

True to his word, Jeremy did come back the next day, and true to Mister Murd's word, he did not particularly care. As soon as the school bell rang, Jeremy made a beeline for Curious Oddities, which once blended inconspicuously into the bodega which housed it, but now shone like a bonfire on a dark night. Opening the door to that same welcoming chime and the same musty smell, Jeremy felt an enthusiastic sort of peace.

Visiting Murd and his house of the bizarre became a regular habit for Jeremy. Unlike the toy store, which was so often filled with screaming, greedy children demanding the latest trend, or overworked employees who made Jeremy feel guilty just for being there, Murd's only ever had a few customers at a time, and the hours after school let out were evidently the slow period. It was quiet here, and there were always new treasures which captivated the imagination.

Sometimes, Jeremy would ask Mister Murd questions about things in the shop, but he never got a straight answer. Murd would often question whether Jeremy intended to buy something or simply continue to loiter, although he never made so much as a veiled threat to remove him from the store. With the yo-yo still on his mind, Jeremy had taken to looking for coins on the ground; pennies and nickels, or even the legendary quarter. He would present Murd with his ever-expanding pile of dirty change and ask if that was enough, and it never was.

There was a consistency to Murd that Jeremy liked. Nearly a decade of cartoons had taught him that people stuck to a specific character model; Fred Flintstone would always be portly and clad in his orange shirt with spots, the Scooby Gang would always be meddling kids and never meddling adults, and so on. *Real* life didn't work like that, though, as people continued to age and get fatter or thinner, or get drastically different haircuts.

Murd, on the other hand, always appeared relatively the same. His head was always balding, with dark hair acting like a coat worn by the combination of his scalp and forehead. There wasn't much variation in his outfit, either, which usually consisted of a shadow gray vest overtop a pale dress shirt and charcoal pants. His tie was a shade between scarlet and crimson which Jeremy's father called the Devil's red, and he wore a small pair of round glasses on his nose which Jeremy thought sometimes made him look like an alien.

Even the constant rejection of Jeremy's money, modest and filthy as it was, provided a kind of sameness which was agreeable to Jeremy. But his desire for the yo-yo, whose repeated image now adorned Jeremy's copy of *Charlie and the Chocolate Factory*, as well as several of his comic books, outweighed his appreciation for routine. On a particularly windy day in September, Jeremy puffed up his chest, approached the front counter, and demanded Mister Murd give him a price for the yo-yo.

“Bring me money that has been hard-earned,” said Edwin Murd after brief deliberation. He had made a feeble show of using an abacus, but the lack of a distinct number made Jeremy think Mister Murd was messing with him.

That night over dinner, Jeremy declared plainly that he wanted to start doing chores around the house and earn an allowance. His parents shared uneasy looks, both remembering how they’d agreed years ago that an allowance for their son wasn’t really in the budget.

“Jeremy…” Kelly Gaunt implored.

“I’ll work really hard!” Jeremy shouted. “And I won’t turn down any work you throw at me, honest.”

Another look shared by the Gaunt parents, this one a little more optimistic, both clearly touched by their son’s passion. They told him they would think about it, an encouraging response but non-committal enough that they could pull out should it prove unfeasible.

But after a hearty discussion in bed during the midnight hours, Alan and Kelly Gaunt put Jeremy to work. Following a week’s worth of dishes, lawn-mowing, and clearing the gutters of autumn leaves, Jeremy was able to enter Curious Oddities with money for the first time.

“Mister Murd, I’d like one yo-yo, please.” Jeremy spoke with equal parts swagger, brought about by his impending victory, and a tremble brought about by the fact that he was exhausted. Newfound energy overwhelmed him, though, when a familiar brown box was once again in sight. The image of the yo-yo peaked through as it opened before bursting forth entirely, the blue star glinting despite the low light.

"Perform with this in front of your friends," Murd explained. "You'll be the most beloved and notorious cretin on the playground."

"Thank you very much!" Jeremy took his prize from the box, a beguiling electricity flowing into his fingers as he touched it. An elegant and sturdy cord wrapped around the midsection of the toy, ending in a gold ring which Jeremy slid around his middle finger. It almost felt like it hugged the chosen digit, elated to be filled as Jeremy wound his arm back.

"Not in here," chided Murd, holding up a finger in disapproval. "You're apt to break something. It's also very important to never lose this trinket; consequences follow those that do."

"Don't worry, Mister Murd; I won't!" Jeremy ran straight home and confined himself in his bedroom to practice. His mother worried her son was sick when he asked to take dinner in his room, but Jeremy had never felt better.

The next day at school, recess could not come soon enough. The kids were initially skeptical that a simple yo-yo could hold their interest. Trading cards and comic books held sway at Bradbury Elementary, with the occasional mania for video games sweeping in. But as soon as the yo-yo first went down, so too did the jaws of Jeremy's entire class.

The way the toy spun blended the red of its body with the blue from its cosmic decoration, giving off spiraling shades of magenta and fuchsia. Jeremy didn't think he was particularly good; his night of practice had only given him a grasp of the most basic tricks. Nevertheless, his fellow students were enraptured, with kids from other classes and grades coming over to see what all the fuss was about.

That was the beginning of a golden week for Jeremy. Everyone wanted to sit with him at lunch, leaving a single table considerably packed and several others completely unoccupied. People laughed at his jokes, and gave him first dibs on new trading cards and collectibles. Even the coolest boy in school, Kurt Marsten, who wore a constant air of snark and apathy, showed Jeremy only the finest social grace. The weekend after was spent sifting through countless invitations to hang outs at other kids' houses.

The following Monday was not so kind.

While getting ready for school, Jeremy became increasingly alarmed as the yo-yo was nowhere to be found. His parents, who had enjoyed the confident glow their son had been wearing for the past several days, were devastated to see Jeremy in such distress, but could provide no insight as to the toy's location. A knot occupied Jeremy's stomach during the morning car ride.

As soon as he arrived, there was a group of kids waiting to see a few yo-yo tricks before first bell. When Jeremy told them the yo-yo was gone, they all seemed to take it personally, wearing looks of utter melancholy as they trudged inside. By the time they took their seats, whatever dejected feelings they held had turned vindictive and spiteful. All day they shot Jeremy dirty looks. When he answered a question incorrectly in class, there rang out a wave of malicious and pointed laughter.

Recess was no easier. Jeremy had planned on avoiding his classmates entirely, but the playground was only so large. When they found him, they approached with a guise of friendship and apology, but once Jeremy's guard was down, they began their harassment in full. Many of their jeers revolved around the phrase 'no-no yo-yo.' They called out his lack of physical ability, something which had not been a problem before the previous week. The worst, though, was how clear and concise they were in expressing their complete and total disdain for him. And even though only a handful of kids took part, surrounding him so running away wasn't an option, most of the others stood by and watched, silently giving their approval of this social execution through inaction.

"I told you not to lose it," Mister Murd told Jeremy, who had come running to his shop after school in tears.

"Please," Jeremy begged. "Do you have another one, Mister Murd? I can get you the money."

"I'm afraid the item was one of a kind," Murd said apathetically. "I got it from a devious pair of carnival folk. I suppose this will just have to be a lesson in protecting your personal property, hmm?"

Jeremy left the shop with renewed tears. When he got home, he threw himself down on his bed, hoping that if he fell asleep now, he could wake up from this nightmare he was experiencing. But as is so often the case with the worst nightmares, it kept going after Jeremy woke up.

As time went on, one school year turning into several, the yo-yo incident was gradually forgotten. But the torment didn't stop, oh no. Children can forget events, but they remember weakness, and in losing that yo-yo against Mister Murd's instruction, Jeremy had somehow shown the purest weakness imaginable. He was prey, his scent telling every jungle beast for miles that he was to be hunted, that his carcass could distract the other wild things from the fact that they were prey too.

Jeremy never stopped visiting Curious Oddities. This was a little baffling for the proprietor, who had found in his experience that patrons rarely returned after feeling the sting of a bad purchase. The ones that did typically sought vengeance, and those that came seeking something from Edwin Murd always paid for it. But not Jeremy Gaunt, who, despite the continuous obloquy that his life had become, did not possess a single mean bone in his body. He was desperate for a friend, and Mister Murd's occasional mocking of his intelligence, which Jeremy had observed every customer receiving in equal measure, was far more preferable to the personalized insults he got at school.

"You know you're the only one I can get to listen to my stories, Mister Gaunt."

“What?” said a thirteen-year-old Jeremy in disbelief. “Didn’t you once tell me you could sell anything to anybody? Why not just use your expert salesman skills?”

“Because, you stupid boy. I don't want to *sell* a story; I want to *tell* a story.”

“I'm starting to suspect people's reluctance to listen to you has nothing to do with your stories.”

“They're two very similar words, you know; sell and tell. Only one letter apart, those letters being alphabetical neighbors. It is pure sloth to settle for the nineteenth letter when the twentieth is the correct one.”

“Do you want to tell me a story or not?”

And this just became the way things were. Jeremy had learned by age fifteen, through significant trial and error, that keeping his head down and swimming with the current, not against it, was the easiest way to survive the insurmountable odds against him in his social life. He threw himself into his hobbies, drawing and reading and watching television. The lack of friends or a social circle to distract him came with the unintended side effect of a steady rise in his grade point average. It wasn’t much, but maybe college could offer him a more positive life experience than whatever this was.

It was his grades that Jeremy had in mind on his way home from school one late October afternoon. It was not uncommon these days for him to skip his visit to Curious Oddities, with the demands of homework growing exponentially every year. Today, though, a brash ambition had overtaken him, its origin found in a glittery piece of black paper clutched in his hand. If he couldn't afford to sacrifice his grades a little, there was no hope for him.

"You want money for Halloween candy?" his mother asked incredulously. "Why? I thought I was making treats like usual?"

"I want something different this time, Mom. Something that's best characteristic isn't 'cost effective.'"

"We could use 'cost effective' this year. Money has been tight."

"Please? I'll make it up to you. Name your price!"

"Alright, alright," eased Kelly Gaunt. While she sometimes lacked insight into how her son was doing, she knew that generally he was unhappy. No friends came by, and he wasn't in any clubs at school; he seemed to lack any human connection besides herself and Alan, except, perhaps, for that strange Edwin Murd fellow. And Jeremy was far from a problem child. He asked for nothing and was grateful for the nothing he received, so if Halloween could somehow lift his spirits, maybe it was worth investing in.

"This is all I can give you," she told him while fetching a coffee can of money off the fridge. "Whatever you buy, I get half of for trick-or-treaters. You can use the rest for whatever you've got planned."

"Thanks, Mom!" Jeremy kissed his mother on the cheek, pocketed the money, and ran out the door. He felt optimistic, more so than he had in a long time. The autumn leaves set loose by the breeze looked like confetti to him, congratulating Jeremy on the merit of his plan. Each scowling and sinister jack-o'-lantern he passed seemed to be beaming with pride just for him.

"Candy..." Mister Murd repeated in a far less congratulatory tone. "You're asking I, Edwin Murd, renowned dealer of wondrous and eldritch objects, the likes of which mankind has only seen in their nightmares, to make you... candy? I won't do it."

"Please? I need something special for the party." Jeremy's voice was firm and tenacious. "If anyone can do that, it's you. I know it isn't your usual thing, but I know you. You're already thinking of ways to do it; you love a challenge."

"That may be true," Murd relented. "But listen here, boy. As one of my few repeat customers, I'll give you the benefit of the doubt by explaining to you how this works. Those who seek to make a purchase from my store do so because there is undoubtedly something they desire which cannot be bought at my store. So tell me, what is it you seek? Just the approval of a few slack-jawed cretins you call your peers?"

The truth was that Jeremy *did* want the approval of his peers, as ridiculous as he knew that to be. Despite the years of name-calling, the abuse, the complete rejection he'd experienced from any sense of belonging or camaraderie, Jeremy still wanted to impress them. But there was one person he wanted to impress more than the others.

Willa Danko had once been one of Jeremy's closest friends. They were a couple of weirdos; they watched the same things on TV, talked the same way, cared about the same things. It was quite possible Jeremy had loved her, as much as one young child can love another. Even after the yo-yo incident, where their entire grade had seemed preternaturally compelled to rebuke Jeremy on every level, she was never cruel or hateful towards him, only distant.

Willa had dyed her hair a vibrant shade of crimson red last year, done in the hopes of drawing the eye away from the mixed blessings of puberty that all the boys, Jeremy included, couldn't stop thinking or talking about. This had earned her the status as something of an outcast, not helped by the fact that Willa preferred to sit alone at lunch and sketch in her notebook over gossiping with the other girls from homeroom. For being oft unwilling to look up from her volume of *Scary Stories to Tell in The Dark* to return the affections of the popular boys, she had received unbridled teasing and harassment.

And Willa loved Halloween more than any time of year.

"So it's about a woman," Murd assessed with unenthused drawl. "What an agonizing cliché."

"Willa is the one throwing the party," Jeremy admitted, holding up a boldly decorated invitation adorned with skulls and bats and pumpkins. "She even gave me this herself. So will you help me, Mister Murd? Please?"

"I don't know..."

“I have money.” Jeremy sheepishly presented what his mother had given him.

“Ten dollars? Hmm.” Murd weighed the five-dollar bill and assortment of change in his palm. After a quick sniff, he seemed satisfied. “Dripping with parental love, has great value in that it is genuinely what little your mother could spare. Faint hint of holiday spirit. Yes, this will do just fine.” He put the money in a small glass bottle, corked it, and placed it on a shelf behind him.

“Fine, I'll grant your request, Jeremy Gaunt. But only because I get dreadfully bored this time of year. With every gas station and malt shop purveying horrors, there's less business that comes my way.”

“What's a malt shop?”

“Just shut up and get me the items off this list.” Murd furiously scrawled on a notepad which bore the words ‘From the desk of Edwin Murd’ on the top. “The Shopper Mart down the street should have it all.”

“Whoa!” Jeremy exclaimed as Murd produced a large roll of bills from his antique cash register. “That's more than double what I paid you. What's different about this cash?”

“Well, it's ordinary; just boring old legal tender. The money your mother gave you represents something, which makes it unique, and that makes it valuable. Now run along and get me all the items on this list, and be quick about it.”

Jeremy did as he was told. He returned forty-five minutes later with two large shopping bags close to bursting. The sign on Murd's front door had been changed to 'Closed' while he was out, but Jeremy let himself in anyway. There was something different about the shop: all the items from the front counter, including the cash register, had been removed. In their place was a large iron bowl which took up the entire left-hand side, and strange symbols had been drawn on with chalk.

"You certainly took your time," Murd said derisively. "Put those bags up here on the counter. Quickly now."

"What is that thing?" Jeremy asked. "Some kind of cooking pot?"

"This, my stupid friend, is a witch's cauldron. It has been passed around by no less than three different covens, each one loading it with distinct curses. Some complement the others; some counteract each other completely. It serves as the first and most important variable of our little experiment.

"I've taken the liberty of marking it with magical sigils and runes from some of my books of forgotten lore." Jeremy could see that half a dozen texts had been pulled off the shelves and lay strewn about the shop. "I have no idea what they mean. They could be dangerous, but therein lies the fun. The chalk I used to scrawl them was made from limestone that came from an Earth alternate to our own. The combination of these three things will provide a tumultuous magical repository for our concoction to stew in."

"What's the cauldron filled with?" The murky liquid inside bubbled as if on a low flame, but there was no apparatus underneath. Jeremy had learned not to question quirks like this when it came to Mister Murd.

"Carbonated soda water. It's a little more interesting than boring, regular water. Now fetch me the first item from my list." Jeremy reached into the shopping bag and pulled out six milk chocolate bars and seven dark chocolate bars. "The number thirteen holds significance to many peoples. Halloween is a night where darkness reigns, so an abundance of dark chocolate is what we need. I want you to put one in after each subsequent ingredient, do you understand?"

Jeremy nodded. He threw a bar in and watched it slowly dissolve, muddying the water.

"Give up the next ingredient, boy." Jeremy produced a large bottle of high fructose corn syrup. Murd unscrewed the cap and let the whole thing pour into the cauldron. "This stuff is found in all sorts of Halloween candy. It carries the essence of the holiday." Jeremy put another bar in.

"You're not really going to put in this black licorice, are you, Mister Murd? Black licorice is the worst Halloween candy out there." The shop owner swiped at the boy violently, grabbing the package and tearing a hole in it. He reached in and put several pieces of the umbral confectionary into his mouth.

"They happen to be for me, you louse."

They found their rhythm after that. Jeremy handed grocery items to Murd one after the other, followed with the adding of a chocolate bar. Items included things like marshmallow fluff and honey that had come from a local beehive. After a certain point, Murd started including items that had not come from Jeremy's recent excursion. A smidge of powdered quartz crystal went in, making the foul-smelling concoction crackle. One tiny bottle emitted a fine mist into the mixture, which Murd explained was the last breath of a hanged man. Next in was a handful of small yellow pellets.

"Eye of newt; a classic." Murd stirred the cauldron, which bubbled and frothed vigorously. The grocery bag nearly empty, Murd called for the penultimate item they contained. "Red ginseng is a natural aphrodisiac." He winked as he threw it into the pot, and Jeremy couldn't help but blush.

"It's getting a little thick, Mister Murd. Shouldn't we add some more water?"

"Right you are, Jeremy Gaunt." From underneath the counter, Murd brought up a water bottle with the label torn off. The water inside was cloudy and unpleasant to look at. "Water from Loch Ness in Scotland. I myself have little doubt that the so-called 'Loch Ness Monster' is anything more than an attractive delusion, but that delusion has captured the hearts and minds of dreamers for over a century! This water is loaded with so much passive psychic energy that there's no telling what it will do!"

This made the cauldron stir far easier than it had before. Jeremy didn't know what to make of the smell at this point, but he trusted that it would taste better once it was ready. Murd held out a hand for the last item, which Jeremy had waiting.

"'Dehydrated pumpkin slices?!'" the man read from the package with building annoyance. "My list specifically said 'a pumpkin,' as in one full gourd!"

"It's October 30th, Mister Murd. They were sold out."

"I suppose there *is* an improvisational component to this endeavor. Fine, this will have to do. Pumpkins are emblematic of the season we find ourselves in, when the veil is thinnest. That connection will draw the holiday spirit to our brew and change it in untold ways."

Jeremy had just assumed most of what Mister Murd said tonight was an exaggeration, but as soon as the slices hit the cauldron, the smell changed drastically. Halloweens past flooded back to him, with the scents of rotting leaves and candle smoke from inside carved pumpkins filling his nose. Candy apples and popcorn and every sugary treat imaginable dominated his thoughts. He was a little boy again, going door to door as a vampire clown and relishing each time an adult called him 'positively terrifying.' Even as his other senses pulled him back to reality, the experience had brought a tear to his eye.

While he was nostalgically incapacitated, the shopkeeper grabbed Jeremy by the back of the head and forced it over the cauldron, his tear falling into the swirling soup. Jeremy pulled away and looked at Murd with shocked anguish.

"We would have been remiss to not harvest such an emotionally charged ingredient."

“Whatever,” Jeremy groaned, rubbing his aggravated scalp. “So is it done now?”

“There’s one last step.” Murd brought out from the shelves behind him two large muffin trays with indents that were decidedly not muffin-shaped.

“What are those, exactly?”

“The icosahedron, you plebian child. Long ago, a wizard named Gygax discovered the power of the icosahedron, and his followers still use it to this day.”

“Wow,” Jeremy sighed while Murd picked up the cauldron and began to pour its contents into the molds. “These candies will be magic, then? What do they do, exactly?”

“I have absolutely no idea.” A wicked smile crept over Murd’s face as he walked the trays over to the refrigerator in his back room. “It’s exciting, isn’t it?”

“They need a name… something that suits them. What about ‘Halloween Surprise’? Because neither of us knows what’ll happen when people eat them?”

“That name is uninspired and ridiculous, but I will accept it for want of a better one. You can pick up your ‘Halloween Surprise’ tomorrow after school. Do not be late.”

Jeremy promised he wouldn’t be. After getting home and falling asleep that night, his dreams were filled with hayrides and hot apple cider and other autumn wonders, but mostly they were filled with Willa Danko.

“What are they exactly?” asked Alan Gaunt after Jeremy got home, holding an edible icosahedron between his thumb and forefinger. “Some kind of chocolate?”

“They’re some kind of everything, I think,” answered his son. It was as honest an answer as he could give.

“I don’t want you eating those, Al,” Kelly warned. “Jeremy’s taking half for his little party tonight, so I want to make sure we have enough for the trick-or-treaters.”

“Yes, dear,” Jeremy’s father relented, placing his scavenged piece of candy back into the carnival glass bowl his wife had set up. “Remind me where you got that funky costume again?”

“Mister Murd gave it to me.” Jeremy’s most recent encounter with his friend had been strange, but his mind was so preoccupied with other things he could not fathom any good reason why.

“I imagine,” Murd had said earlier, “that you’ve neglected to procure a costume for the celebration this evening, given that you haven’t been blathering on about one?”

“Oh, shoot!” Jeremy yelled.

“Calm yourself, boy. I took the liberty of acquiring this for you. No, don’t worry, it isn’t an item from my shop; you should be so lucky. A local drugstore provided this garb. Happy Halloween, Jeremy Gaunt.”

"'The Fool,'" Jeremy read off the packaging. "I don't get it."

"You will."

"Well, that was nice of him," Jeremy's mother said back in the present. "Now let's get you to that party; I want to be back before the first kid rings our doorbell."

The Danko household was found on the corner of Elm Street and Ocean Avenue. It was painted a bright canary yellow, but in the late October darkness and the light of store-bought decorations, it came off as the color of long and sickly toenails. Jeremy could hear loud music as he approached the door, and for a brief moment he considered turning around right then and there. Before he could decide on the best course of action, the decision was made for him.

"Are you here for candy or the party?" asked a tiny skeleton wearing a horned helmet and faux fur pelt.

"Uhm, the party?"

"What do you have to offer the Sentinel Skeleton to gain entry?" the boy demanded. Jeremy reached into his paper bag and produced a single unit of his Halloween Surprise. The skeleton took it in his observably flesh-covered hand, sniffed it, and then added it to a plastic jack-o'-lantern on an end table next to him.

"Okay, you can come in," the skeleton said pleasantly, who lifted his skull to reveal a bright-eyed ten-year-old underneath. "I'm Willa's brother, Michael. Please respect our house."

Jeremy gave an affable nod and pushed passed him. The inside of the house was dimly lit. It was divided in two with a stairwell in the middle. The left-hand side led into a small sitting room, which was blocked off along with the stairs by a coatrack for guests, an armchair, and the Sentinel Skeleton's little table. On the righthand side was a more open living room where lights flashed, and a techno remix of Ghostbusters played through bass-boosted speakers. Jeremy took a deep breath, a difficult feat considering he had begun to hyperventilate, and made his way over.

There was no particular theme to the dancing, unless you considered 'discord' a theme. Jeremy saw an astronaut and a caveman doing the robot together, a Raggedy Anne who was grinding on a Raggedy Andy, and a particularly tall boy with red hair dressed as a leprechaun did some kind of jig at a speed which did not look comfortable, as many onlookers cheered for him to go faster. A couch and a loveseat had been pushed up against different walls, but both were filled with people having conversations which could not be heard over the music. Jeremy drifted about awkwardly until he saw there was a brightly lit kitchen further in the house.

His first step in was hesitant and calculated. Jeremy knew from pop culture and one failed attempt at attending a house party last year that the kitchen was where people came to chat, when the luminous darkness of the dancefloor didn't interest them. He was afraid of being too conspicuous and drawing every eye in the room at once.

"Now I know you're not dressed as a freak, Gaunt," came a confident voice from around a corner. "Because you're already that every other day of the year. So what the hell are you supposed to be tonight?"

"Hi, Kurt," Jeremy croaked, doing his best to keep his voice even and emotionless. "Hubie, Susan. How're you guys doing?"

"Oh, fine," Susan Mears drawled in that cheerleader sort of way that was purposefully vague in tone. She was dressed in a doctor's uniform with a white wig that appeared frazzled and crazy. The top three buttons of her shirt were undone, and it took every last bit of Jeremy's willpower to avoid letting his gaze drift below her face.

"I asked you a question," Kurt Marsten reiterated, his Frankenstein costume making his broad frame even more intimidating. Unlike his girlfriend Susan, Kurt's tone was very clear: I'm a fun and friendly guy, but I could break you if I decide you have it coming.

"Yeah, the man asked you a question, Gaunt. You don't want to be rude, do you?" Hubie Barlow had been Kurt's friend, or perhaps more accurately, his sidekick, since the third grade. He wore a dollar-store grim reaper cloak, with a couch cushion shoved down the back serving as Igor's hump. Hubie suffered from a Napoleon-adjacent complex ever since coming to the realization that the coveted growth spurt received by many teen boys during puberty wasn't coming. Jeremy sometimes felt sorry for him, but then he remembered the time Hubie had thrown a dodgeball right into his testicles during gym class while he was already on the ground.

"He's clearly 'The Fool,'" a soft voice from behind them shouted. "One of the major arcana from a tarot deck. Maybe you'd know stuff like that if you didn't cut class to smoke behind the dumpsters so often."

"I don't smoke!" whined Susan.

"Oh, honey," said Willa Danko. "All the second-hand fumes you get from your boyfriend and his ventriloquist dummy are just as bad. Now will you three please stop harassing my guest?"

One by one they gave Jeremy dirty looks as they pushed passed him. Kurt bid him farewell with a hard slap to the paper bag he was holding. If not for Jeremy's anxious crumpling of the top half for the past five minutes, the bag's contents would have spilled completely onto the floor. He crouched down to pick it up, but another hand brushed up against his. His skin felt hot, and he looked up to see Willa Danko on the floor with him.

Jeremy bit his tongue to avoid letting out a yelp and shot to his feet. He couldn't take his eyes off Willa as she stood. She wore a skin-tight green leotard with a bold leaf print, and emerald dancers' tights with a thorny vine drawn around the legs in sharpie. Around her arms and shoulders, she wore a plastic jungle vine which had been spray-painted black. Topping it all off was a headpiece which resembled a daisy, or possibly a white rose, and glittery makeup which shone in the fluorescent lighting. She looked radiant, and Jeremy had to fight to keep his wits about him.

"Do you like my costume?" she asked before doing a spin. "It started off as Poison Ivy, but then I found the flower and it sort of became a Mother Nature type thing."

"Y-Yeah, you look beautiful."

"Well, thank you," Willa beamed. "Sorry about those guys. Did they hurt your... what's in the bag? It isn't drugs, is it?"

"What?!" Jeremy screeched. "No, no. It's candy, homemade."

Willa's eyes went wide. "Oh my gosh, you're a lifesaver." She took the bag from him exuberantly. "My dad didn't buy enough snacks and we're nearly out. I was worried we'd have a real monster mash on our hands, y'know?"

"Heh, yeah." Jeremy watched as she pulled out a piece of candy and sniffed it much in the same way her brother had.

"These are interesting," she said with an intrigued grin. "I dig the shape. What are they, chocolate?"

"I call them Halloween Surprise. They're a totally unique treat."

Willa took a bite and chewed. The look on her face went through several stages, starting with inquisitive assessment, transitioning into wide-eyed and vivid astonishment. It concluded with a sort of childlike glee, as her lips were pulled into a smile that was almost too big for her face.

"Oh my gosh, you made these things?" she exclaimed, popping two more in her mouth.

"You could say I guided the overall process, yeah." Jeremy's face had become so hot that it took him a while to realize he was smiling too. Seeing his crush excitedly pour his creation into a serving bowl made him happy, but it was also deeply satisfying on a level he couldn't describe.

"Hey, everyone!" Willa shouted to her party guests. "Jeremy brought you all more candy!" A loud roar escaped the living room as no less than fifteen monsters and sports stars and vague sexy animals filed into the kitchen. The bowl was seized from Willa and passed around the drunk crowd. Some came up to Jeremy and pumped their fists boisterously. A few even patted him on the back while slurring some unintelligible thanks or approval. When the first few people tasted the Halloween Surprise they began to cheer, "Jer-Em-Y! Jer-Em-Y!" They didn't stop even as they moved back into the living room.

"You're a hit!" Willa shouted excitedly, chuckling pleasantly at Jeremy's bewilderment.

"Yeah, I think I might cry." Jeremy laughed to make it seem like he was joking, but the first positive reinforcement he'd received from people his own age in years was an uncanny feeling.

"Hey, you draw, right?"

"Excuse me?"

"I wasn't watching you or anything," she said defensively. "But you're not exactly subtle about how you're always sketching in class. I saw some of your drawings when you dropped your notes after history last week."

Silently, Jeremy cursed his own lack of dexterity or grace. He was used to retroactively criticizing his own actions and mistakes; the reflex was always primed and ready to fire.

"They were really good!" The words hung in the air, refracting time in the kitchen so what was only a brief pause in speaking felt to Jeremy like far longer. "A lot of them looked like they were anime inspired, right?"

"Yeah, actually."

And that was how Jeremy's conversation with Willa began. What amazed him the most was just how easy it was. Despite the years-long gap in their communication, in spite of his immeasurable self-doubt when it came to his own charisma, talking to Willa just felt right. While he still had the same carnal fantasies that were stereotypical of teens his age, his deeper longing was for a friend he could connect with. The more they talked about the books they'd read or the terrible movies they enjoyed, the less Jeremy felt alone.

It was while they were discussing their mutual love for Edgar Allan Poe that Willa asked Jeremy if he wanted to see something cool. She looked around to make sure no other guests were watching them before taking Jeremy's hand and leading him towards the front of the house.

"It's easier if we just climb," she told him before scaling the armchair which blocked the stairs. After trying and failing to avoid staring at her backside on the way over, Jeremy followed suit. The upper floor of the Danko household was dark; Willa had told Jeremy that her parents were out for the evening. They had passed Michael downstairs, keeled over, presumably, from too much candy. They went by two closed doors before looping around to a third with a painted wooden 'W' on it.

Willa's bedroom was a bright shade of violet. Most of her furniture, from her bookshelves to her bed frame, was painted a striking onyx black. On the walls were posters for the original *Friday the 13th* and *Kiki's Delivery Service*. The feature that stood out most, however, was an elevated birdcage by the window which overlooked the front lawn. Inside was a raven, which eyed the pair curiously.

"Poor thing crashed into the side of our house. Dad wanted to put it out of its misery, but I asked if I could try to nurse him back to health. That was weeks ago. He's just about ready to fly. I was going to release him after the party tonight."

"Willa, that's amazing," said Jeremy in awe. His face was up close to the cage, and Willa's had come up just next to his. When they mutually recognized their closeness, they both blushed, but neither pulled away, the building heat between them compelling them to do the opposite. They got closer and closer until their lips touched climactically.

Time refracted again for Jeremy. There was a giggle, followed by awkward silence, followed by the two of them moving to Willa's bed. To Jeremy, this all happened in the span of a few seconds, and before he knew it, their lips were locked in a fiery embrace. His hand was on her thigh, hers on his chest. His body was a chemical engine working in overdrive, so much so that he did not notice a peculiar gurgling sound which filled the room.

"Whoa," moaned Willa, pulling back with an uncomfortable look on her face.

"I'm sorry!" Jeremy cried, backing away immediately. "Did I do something wrong?"

"No," she winced. "You're great. I think I just need to go to the bathroom. Be right back."

She got up and went into an attached bathroom opposite her bed. The door closed and Jeremy sweat nervously. His perception was slowly catching up with his hormones, and it had trouble believing what was happening. His thoughts spiraled, wondering if whatever curse he was under had finally been lifted. If he could lock lips with a girl like Willa Danko, it had to be, didn't it?

An eerie orange glow pulled him back to the present moment. Jeremy looked around in alarm and saw that it was coming from Willa's bathroom door. He approached slowly, calling Willa's name. He thought he could hear her groaning, but whether it was a cry for help or dismissal of his concerns, he could not tell. He put his ear up to the door, afraid of violating her privacy but concerned for her safety too.

And then the bathroom exploded.

A single burst splintered the door and sent Jeremy flying backwards. He lost consciousness, but only for a few seconds. The raven's cage was likewise knocked over, and the trapped bird shrieked furiously. When Jeremy awoke, he could hear sounds of confusion coming from downstairs. He himself had trouble piecing together what was going on. He saw the bathroom, which was smoldering from whatever had caused the blast.

He peaked inside, but immediately retreated and threw up on the heather gray carpet in Willa's room. The tiled floor of the bathroom had been cracked in three places, and shattered glass was thrown about from where the vanity mirror had been pulverized. The sink itself was on the floor, and a jet of water bounced off the ceiling, creating indoor rainfall. It carried away significant amounts of blood, which coated every surface.

Jeremy couldn't bring himself to look at Willa Danko, or at least what was left of her; it wasn't physically possible to look in that many directions at once.

"Halloween Surprise..." he muttered to himself, his mind building to a horrific realization. As if on cue, another explosion came from downstairs. Somebody screamed, and the music cut off abruptly. Then another explosion. And another. They came in rapid succession, each one rocking the house more and more.

Panic set in when Jeremy realized the structural integrity of the house was at risk. Another explosion and he felt the very room he was in lurch in one direction. He fought with the window to open, but it was locked in a way he wasn't familiar with. The raven cawed, which gave Jeremy a rash idea.

He picked up its cage and turned it on its side, using the bottom of it like a battering ram to shatter the window. The raven objected miserably but was shielded from any broken glass. One final explosion and the floor began to go out from under him. He leapt, cage still in hand, and touched down hard on the lawn below.

The bones in his right leg shattered instantly. His pain was intense, but adrenaline created an odd sort of calm, the eye in a hurricane of agony. Willa's house crumpled behind him, causing the last few trick-or-treaters to scatter and wail. The raven flew off, its cage bent open just enough in the fall. It was then Jeremy saw the night sky come alive with flashing orange lights. The last thing he remembered before going into shock was the candy he had given to his mother to hand out, and the last thing he heard was the night fill with explosions and mortified screams.

Across town, Edwin Murd watched the carnage unfolding through his shop window. "So that's what they do," he observed, unsurprised but nevertheless satisfied. He deftly changed the sign in his window from 'Come in, we're Open' to 'Sorry, we're Closed.' His usual post behind the front counter called to him, and he grabbed a handful of black licorice. With his other hand he removed from his pocket a red yo-yo emblazoned with a blue star, and bobbed it up and down playfully.

“God, I love Halloween,” he mused. With a big smile on his face, he bit into his licorice, and Edwin Murd enjoyed his sweets thoroughly.

The October Carnival

"We appear without a sound, the darkest show around." -Creature Feature, "The Greatest Show Unearthed"

The town of Whisper Falls would not be celebrating Halloween this year. It was a decision which had been almost universally reviled, but still the city council held firm. The decision could be traced back to last Halloween, during which no less than three tragedies took place. To some, it was a comfort to believe they were all related, with one malevolent trickster being the cause. The alternative was to accept that the wickedness which persisted in their town was legion, or simply that the random chance of the Universe could allow such misfortune at any time.

The first tragedy was the least complicated. Ray Brady, aged eleven, had disappeared without a trace. He had been eager to go out with his friends to get candy, his parents reported, but neither of them had been available to drive him. Despite their firm instruction that he was to stay home and watch Halloween specials on TV, he had set out to make the journey himself on foot. None of his friends had seen him, meaning something had happened to him along the way. Whether he had been snatched in the night or merely vanished into thin air, not a soul could say.

The second tragedy was the second most harmful. Multiple groups of teenagers had independently decided to make a name for themselves as master pranksters, making an innocent bet with one another when their activities overlapped to see who could pull off the most elaborate pranks by midnight. What was surely just a nuisance at first turned into a malicious game of one-upmanship, which ended in three hospitalizations, dozens of police reports, and thousands of dollars in property damage. No arrests were made and no reprisals were dealt out on account of every perpetrator wearing a mask.

While not counted amongst the tragedies which occurred that October 31st, it is worth noting that those involved in the prank wars had all simultaneously removed their costumes and discarded them in a river which ran through the heart of the town. The decision was hasty, conceived from a mixture of exhaustion, fear of consequence, and a nasty sugar rush which rivalled the fiercest intoxication. The buildup of fabric and cheap plastic clogged the waterways, causing flooding in several areas and killing off a population of salmon which was in the middle of its annual migration.

And then there was the final tragedy. A batch of tainted candy, homemade, had poisoned dozens of trick-or-treaters. Had the matter ended there it would have been one thing, but there was an additional side-effect to these treats, one which caused those who consumed them to, well... the less said about it, the better. Suffice it to say, one suburban household was destroyed, and countless sidewalks were irrevocably stained from the evening's carnage.

The media fallout was heinous, with everyone falling over themselves with the sheer volume of ways to ask how such an awful night was allowed to happen. Fingers were pointed, and names were thrown under the bus by those looking for someone to blame. The small town whose most exciting export was drywall suddenly found itself on the national news, with words like 'irresponsible' and 'cataclysmic' thrown in, because what's a wound without a little salt to liven things up a little?

The idea of canceling Halloween was floated around for several weeks before the motion carried. There may have been more opposition to it, had it not been for the collective trauma of Whisper Falls. Nobody wanted to even think about Halloween, and any reminders served only to turn their eyes away. They distracted themselves with preparations for Christmas, but that December which should have been warmed by festive lights and good cheer was just cold.

There weren't even that many on the city council who wanted to cancel Halloween. But there were eyes on them, and they were expected to do *something* to show they were trying to prevent another disaster. By the time it got far enough to actually happen, it was too late; if they backed down now it would make them look weak, and open the town up to more scrutiny. When the decision was made, each politician involved privately absolved themselves of guilt with potent denial, maintaining that cancelling the holiday was really the best thing for their community.

Local businesses felt the hit coming first. Stock which had been ordered almost a year in advance had to be sent back at cost to the retailers. Hefty fines were issued to anyone promoting Halloween or trick-or-treating. Any candy packaged in seasonally dark wrapping, or costumes of any kind, were targets on the back of every small grocer and big box store. A few thought they could still make a profit by accepting these fines and selling festive merchandise anyway, but there was no one heretical enough to buy it.

It had been a gray September in more ways than one that year. Heavy rainfall beat down on Whisper Falls, painting the sky in bleak tones which mirrored the way more and more people seemed to feel. Christmas music came early from a few stores; a fitting death knell for the holiday that kids loved, and most adults didn't realize they'd miss until it was gone.

"I can't take it anymore!" shouted Becky Myers, aged thirteen. Had there been anyone present besides her two best friends, she might have felt a little more insecure about such an unbridled and spirited display of passion. But there wasn't, so she just felt ticked off.

"Easy, fearless leader," offered Joe. "People our age shouldn't have blood pressure as high as yours."

"Or forehead veins as large," added Avery, their words slightly muffled by a sizable piece of red licorice.

"I don't care!"

Becky took the banning of Halloween a bit harder than most. The whole thing had been spearheaded by her mother, the mayor, despite it being a time her daughter lived for. She grounded Becky for a month last January when she staged a formal protest at her school in opposition of the ban. Currently, she was staring daggers at Becky from outside a police car window.

"Rebecca Lee Myers, I cannot believe you would embarrass me like this."

"The feeling is mutual."

"Don't get smart."

"She does that, ma'am." Both Avery and the two Myers women shot Joe reproachful looks.

"What were you thinking?" the mayor continued. "Showing up outside my office—"

"It's city hall, Mom. Public property."

"Outside my office with those ridiculous signs. I suppose this was your secret 'social studies homework' that you've been working on in your room all week."

"It *is* social studies, Mom. We're trying to spark social change and appeal the decisions made by our incompetent local government."

"Where did you even get those costumes?" demanded Becky's mother, ignoring her daughter's barbed comment. "Nobody should be selling them."

"There're still a few places! I guess we just care more about supporting local businesses than you do."

"Alright, that's enough." The mayor pinched the bridge of her nose in frustration. "You're just lucky Officer Addams saw you before too many other people did."

"Thanks again, Dad. Real supportive!" Avery called into the front seat.

"Child, you will show the mayor some respect and let her finish speaking. We'll talk at home, and that is less a threat and more a promise." There was something just a trifle unsettling about a parent who could scold their progeny while keeping an even tone. Even the mayor got goosebumps.

"More people should have seen us, though." Becky's eyes got bigger as she tried to hold back the coming tears. "Mom, this town needs Halloween. I know you love this time of year almost as much as I do. All those spooky movies we watched with Dad, the pumpkin patches and hayrides, the haunted house you organized the year I turned ten! Isn't that stuff worth preserving? That feeling?"

"I..." she trailed off. Avery's father hadn't turned around to address them when he spoke before, but even he had to allow himself a glance back in anticipation of how the mayor would respond.

"Officer Addams is going to drive you home." There was a slight quiver in her voice as she spoke. "When you get there, you will stay in your room until further notice, or so God help me there will be hell to pay."

"But—"

"And that is the end of the conversation! I need to go explain to the press why my daughter was protesting my office while dressed as a witch."

"A necromancer," Becky corrected, no longer making eye contact with her mother.

"Thank you again, Charlie," she said to Avery's father, while resuming her dagger stare into the backseat. "I trust you have it from here."

"That I do, mayor. And you're welcome."

As they drove away, tears fell down Becky's face. She refused to sob, her hands clutching themselves to whitening in her lap and her face aimed squarely at her shoes. Joe and Avery each attempted a comforting gesture, but the young necromancer recoiled from their touch.

"For what it's worth," said Officer Addams, "and your mother will have my badge if she catches wind of me telling you this, so as a courtesy I'm trusting you to keep it zipped, but I admire what you were trying to do, kid." Becky only sniffled in response.

"Going out there and standing up for what you believe in, standing up to your kin, no less, that takes guts. Does my heart good to know my Avery is hanging around good people."

"Dad..." groaned Avery.

"But if you ask me, and I know you're not asking, just relax, you've gotta learn to pick your battles. You can be a dragon, but a dragon spitting into the wind is apt to get their face burned."

"What?" croaked Joe in a comedically exaggerated voice.

"I'm saying that if you take on the world, you might wind up just hurting yourself. Rebecca— sorry, Becky. Your mom loves you, and I know you love her. Do you really want this whole Halloween nonsense to be the thing that drives you two apart? Is it that important?"

"I d-don't know," she said honestly.

"And that's okay. You're thirteen. If ever there was a time in your life to not know something, it's now. I'm just saying, it's worth thinking about. Ain't no shame in admitting when you're beat."

"Like how you've been passed up for sergeant six times now, Dad?"

"Watch it, child," said the officer, annoyed but still lovingly.

No one spoke for the rest of the car ride. At some point, Becky leaned into Avery's shoulder, relenting and letting them put their arm around her. She reached out her hand for Joe to take, which he did, and she cried fully. Officer Addams watched the scene play out in his rear-view mirror, his heart warmed and broken in equal measure.

The weeks rolled on, gray September turning into an October of flamboyant orange. Any mandates or bans on holiday attire didn't apply to the trees, it seemed. Becky was grateful that something still looked like October in her hometown, less so that she was required to rake it up for her whole street as part of her punishment.

In the middle of tying up her sixth trash bag of leaves, something sticking out of the top caught her eye. It was thin and orange like a leaf, but upon closer inspection, Becky realized she had raked up some kind of flyer. It had a spiderweb pattern on one side and tabs cut in the bottom that people could rip off, each one printed with 'ADMIT ONE' in all caps.

'The Gonzo Brothers,' read the flyer's curvy onyx text, 'are proud to bring you their world-famous travelling circus and carnival, one night only! Rides! Games! Freaks and Horrors! And come see the world-premiere of the newest addition to our menagerie!' The date on the bottom read October 30th. In the righthand corner above the tabs was a logo, a realistic skull with a bat flying out of one eye. 'Gonzo Industries. Delight, Entertain, Terrify' was written underneath.

Becky looked around as if she were a spy in possession of state secrets, checking to make sure no one was watching her. Satisfied that she worked in relative obscurity, she folded the flyer and carefully pocketed it. Her work resumed, and later that night she would hide the flyer under her mattress for safekeeping.

Whisper Falls earned its name that month, with the flyers that had mysteriously popped up all over town being gossiped about in hushed tones and careful murmurs. City hall put together a group of volunteers to take them down en masse. The mayor considered having her daughter take part, but by this point her punishment had concluded.

Besides, while the flyer did not specifically advertise a Halloween celebration, it was close enough in date and subject matter that Becky's mother felt it would be unwise to have her involved. Her office never publicly acknowledged the flyers, merely putting out a public statement reminding citizens that Halloween was still banned.

"So we're for sure going, right?" Becky asked her friends.

"For the ninth time, yes," said Avery.

"I just want to be sure."

"I mean," Joe looked around while speaking. "We're already on our way. What did you have to tell your mom to get out tonight?"

"Ha!" Becky smiled. "She's busy with work. As far as she's concerned, I'm still in my room sulking."

"It looks like half the town is on their way to this thing," observed Avery. Like them, many citizens of Whisper Falls made their way on foot towards the location described in the flyer— an empty field on the outskirts of town. Asphalt gave way to dirt road about a mile out, making the walk a feasible one. Feasible, if not for the occasional car passing them by kicking up clouds of dust and exhaust.

After ten minutes of walking, they saw a beacon of light in the distance cut through the darkness of late dusk. There had been some doubt in their minds that there would actually be a carnival at the end of this, that the flyers weren't some kind of elaborate prank or protest. It seemed they were not the only skeptical ones, as a small crowd had formed at the top of the hill which led down into the field. No one spoke to each other, the shared moment of awe enough to bind them all.

“Race ya.” It was a teenaged boy who broke the silence, speaking to no one in particular before darting down the hill with his arms stretched out like an airplane. Inspired by his example, Becky smiled and shot forward as well. Joe and Avery looked at one another, shrugged, and did the same. The rest of the group, some kids and some adults, followed suit.

While this field had hosted a plethora of county fairs, festivals, and the occasional community barbecue, there was no formal parking lot, so cars sat motionless at odd angles every few feet. A chain link fence had been erected which blocked off the entrance to the carnival. Becky wondered if it went around the whole field as her and her friends joined the crowd waiting anxiously for entry.

“I bet you any money he's the ticket taker,” Becky said to her friends, gesturing towards the silhouetted carny a few feet inside the fence. “These operations always have one.”

“I don't believe it,” said a voice which made Becky's blood run cold. “Rebecca, what are you doing here?”

“Oh. Hi, Mom.” Her shoulders immediately slumped when faced with the mayor. “Here for the circus?”

“Hardly. I’m getting to the bottom of these shenanigans. You didn’t walk all the way here by yourself, did you?

“I...”

“Not so, mayor,” said Officer Addams, appearing from behind the crowd. “I see my Avery there with her. Looks like Joseph Prince too. Your dad know you're out this late, Joe?"

"He knows," came a voice from just outside their circle. Owen Prince clasped a disapproving hand on his son's shoulder, stuffing the reporter's notebook he was carrying back into his pocket. "I guess this is a group outing now."

Before Mayor Myers could reprimand them further, a sudden and thunderous slamming of metal echoed through the night. Avery's father unholstered his gun on instinct. When the screams died down, people noticed that the entire chain-link fence had collapsed; not simply falling over, but completely dismantled in an instant.

"Ladies and gentleman!" shouted a man from what had once been the other side of the fence. "The Gonzo Brothers wish to welcome you to the darkest show in town, one night only. Inside, your every wish is our command," he took a dramatic bow, tipping the boater hat he wore atop a mask which made his face look disfigured, "and your every desire is made manifest. Wonders and horrors the likes of which you have never seen await you. I will be your ticket taker this evening."

"Told ya," Becky whispered.

"Please step inside and enjoy!" The Ticket Taker gestured with a glass cane that picked up the changing lights from inside the carnival. "Step lively, now. Form an orderly line. Or push and shove; I'm not a cop."

"No, but I am," said Charlie, using his badge and stature to get to the front. The other five followed behind him, led by the mayor.

"I'm Mayor Olivia Myers," she said confidently, doing her best to exude an air of authority.

"My first patrons of the night!" chirped the Ticket Taker. "How exciting!"

"I want to know what you people are doing here. Where are your permits? Who authorized you to be here?"

"I'm afraid I'm just a humble ticket taker," said the man, his stubbly chin contorting into an exaggerated frown. Becky adored his outfit, apparently composed piecemeal from a wardrobe's worth of garish attire.

"You can flag down our illustrious hosts, the Gonzo Brothers, once you get inside. But no one gets inside without a ticket. That's kind of my one rule."

"Sweet, we're going in," Becky declared triumphantly. She produced the flyer from her coat pocket and held it above her head for all to see.

"Oh no we're not," said her mother. She grabbed for the flyer, but underestimated her daughter's grip and tore the paper in two.

"Mom!" Becky shrieked. Quickly she assessed the state of her treasure, content that there were still usable tabs but nevertheless shaken. "This sucks, you know that? Halloween was the one thing I could look forward to every year, but thanks to you it's gone."

"Becky..."

"And now this carnival comes along, one last chance for Whisper Falls to have a little fun before winter, and your first thought is to stop it? Well, you can try, but I'm going in before you ruin this too like you ruin everything else!"

Olivia Myers had so much she wanted to say to her daughter in that moment, conflicting thoughts tying her tongue. Before she found the right words, if she ever could, she was caught off guard by the sound of whistling and raucous applause from the line which had formed behind them. In the seconds it took her to find her composure, her daughter had presented three stubs to the Ticket Taker and rushed inside with her friends.

"Becky, wait!" Her pursuit was cut short before it could even begin, as the cane of the Ticket Taker came down like the gate of a tollbooth.

"Tickets please," he said with a smirk. Olivia looked at her half of the flyer, which bore exactly three tabs on it.

"Charlie, Owen, I hate to ask you this, but could you...?"

"You sign my cheques, Liv." Avery's father gave the mayor a reassuring smile. "Plus, that's my kid in there too, so I'm in."

"I was going in anyway," said Owen. "But I forgot to bring a flyer, so this works out just fine for me."

Beyond the threshold of the carnival, Becky, Avery, and Joe stood transfixed at the onslaught of sights and sounds the night lay before them. Booths of games and snacks and rides were arranged in a spiral pattern, starting with a big top striped in red and black. The children studied the attractions as best they could from their limited vantage point, and reasoned that the spiral ended with a Ferris wheel at the opposite end of the grounds from the entrance.

"We've gotta ride that thing before we go," Becky exclaimed, eyes literally and figuratively twinkling with excitement.

"If our parents don't kill us first," muttered Avery.

"How do you think they get these lights to work?" asked Joe. Becky and Avery had been so fixated on taking in everything, only Joe had seen the details. Strange orbs of light hung about in a milky green vapor. The carnival was covered in them.

"Projector?" Avery suggested. "Casting shapes onto the fog?"

"There'd have to be projectors everywhere, then."

"Yeah, isn't this place amazing?" Becky laughed, not fully hearing her friends. "Check this thing out!" She led them to a raised platform made of finely cut pine, which sat twenty feet in front of the big top. Unlike everything else in the carnival, it was the only structure not a part of the spiral. A black tarp covered something on top, and the only staircase it had was guarded by an older man wearing an ash-colored trench coat over a pair of filthy jean overalls.

"Run along, children," he said in a thin Welsh accent. "You have a world of games and rides to occupy you this evening; you need not bother me with your nonsense."

Becky narrowed her eyes at him, fully prepared to give him a piece of her mind as only a thirteen-year-old can, but a sudden commotion behind her took a hold of her attention. A wave of guests was making its way inside, including her mother near the front. Without much of a plan, she beckoned for her friends to get lost in the shuffle with her.

There was a vibrant energy to the crowd. People looked livelier; they wore their smiles wider than they had in months. There was laughter and cheer, which Becky had forgotten about. Children ran around seeing the sights, and parents chased after them happily. It was as close to a perfect moment as Whisper Falls had seen in a long time.

"Ladies and gentleman!" boomed a voice which emanated from all around. It was loud enough it could have come from concert speakers, but it lacked any of the electric reverb one would expect.

"Thank you so much for joining us this evening!" said a nearly identical but distinct voice. "The Gonzo Brothers wish to welcome you!"

"And welcome you we shall!" The fog permeating the fairgrounds thickened, taking on a faint emerald hue and starting to move as if blown about by several opposing fans. Two disparate tendrils of green smoke wormed around like snakes, meeting at the platform and spiraling up a pole in the back before bursting into fireworks at the top.

No one from Whisper Falls was sure what they were seeing. As the mist cleared, two pale figures stood where the fireworks had gone off, seemingly both balancing atop the tiny beam. They wore identical jackets made from cherry red fabric, which sparkled wickedly in the circus light and was trimmed in dull gold. The man on the left wore his dark hair a little longer, and on his head he wore a rufous red top hat covered in jagged geometric shapes. The man on the right wore a top hat as well, which was the color of smoke and bore vertical stripes. They sported matching bow ties which were blacker than pitch.

"Hello, Whisper Falls!" they greeted in unison.

"That's Chip," said the black hat.

"He's Flim," said the red. "And together we are,"

"The Gonzo Brothers!" The crowd cheered boisterously in response.

"For those of you that don't know us," exposited Flim, "we are a pair of world-class, world-travelling showmen! Isn't that right, brother?"

"It is!" stressed Chip. "And in our travels, we heard tell of one poor, unfortunate town in the heartland U.S. of A. that was going without Halloween this year."

"Unthinkable!"

"So, we packed up our merry band of freaks and misfits—"

"Our carnies and our crooks—"

"And we set out straight away to give you a whole month's worth of fun in just a single night!"

More applause, this time thoughtful and aware. Somewhere in the crowd, Olivia Myers rolled her eyes.

"We have exceptionally fun games," started Chip.

"And rides which will equally thrill and chill you!" continued Flim. "But let's not forget the big top and our circus of horrors held therein. Are we forgetting anything, Chip?"

"We are! You didn't tell them about the menagerie!"

"You mean the one full of monsters, madmen, and everything in between?"

"That's the one!" Chip bellowed enthusiastically. "The one with the brand-new addition we just picked up."

"But we haven't told them about the new addition yet," Flim pointed out.

"We can do that now, if that's agreeable to you."

"Yes, let's!" And then the Gonzo Brothers took a casual, mirrored step off their thirty-foot perch.

The fall was too slow for grown men of their size, but that didn't stop people from screaming after that first step. Becky's brain worked like a colony of ants trying to figure out how they did it. What sold the effect was how they were accelerating in their descent, hitting the ground with a significant impact which kicked up a gust of wind. Ever the showmen, the Gonzos made sure the air blew the tarp off the platform.

The crowd gasped. Underneath the shroud was an old-fashioned pillory. Becky recognized the contraption from history class, the textbook diagram having inspired more than one daydream about how to get back at a few cruel classmates. But there were no children in this pillory, or any human beings at all for that matter. Instead, it housed a scarecrow.

The figure was hunched over, but Becky reckoned from her vantage point that it would be about eight feet tall were it to stand to its full height. Its clothing was a ragged plaid shirt with black overalls. It had a lit jack-o'-lantern for a head, on top of which was a hat that seemed crossbred from a fedora and a classic witch's hat. Its face pointed out and downward so it looked at the crowd. The light inside flickered faintly.

"Isn't he handsome, folks?" sneered Flim.

"This is our good friend Spirit," explained Chip. "Spirit O'Halloween. We encountered him on our jaunt into your neck of the woods."

"Poor bastard was so weak,"

"So emaciated and hopeless. See, Easter has the rodent, Valentine's has the filthy cherub,"

"Christmas has that fat, jolly idiot." The crowd laughed, and the Gonzos shared a look of mutual satisfaction.

"But Halloween here has Spirit," explained Chip. "There have been other contenders and pretenders, pumpkin kings and skeleton shades, et cetera. But they are not THE Spirit O'Halloween."

"Spirit O'Halloween, who got within three counties of this quaint little burg and positively plotzed!"

Becky had been drawn in by the hypnotic quality of the Gonzo Brothers' words so thoroughly that she had nearly forgotten the scarecrow was there. When she looked at it again, it came off as sad, or even sick, and she didn't see before that there were chains around it. The idea that something was wrong seized her slowly, chilling her blood.

"Congratulations, Whisper Falls. You miserable humbugs literally almost killed Halloween!" Flim Gonzo never lost his upbeat cadence, so this remark actually earned a small applause before people began looking around for some direction on how they should be feeling.

"But no matter," Chip assured. "Spirit will have a home with us in our menagerie."

"And seeing as that'll leave a vacancy on the 31st, we've signed our residence applications in triplicate!"

"After tonight, Halloween will be no more!"

"A relic of a bygone era!"

"And in its wake, you'll see a brand-new holiday: Gonzo Day! Run, owned, and operated by us!"

"All rights reserved," Flim noted sternly.

"And because we want you fine folks to enjoy Gonzo Day as much as we do," Chip winked.

"Concessions are on us!" The two brothers held up their arms, and coins shot out of their sleeves like a hemorrhaging wishing well. People swarmed for them the second the first token hit the ground.

"Hold on a minute!" cried a shrill voice from within the crowd. It made enough of an impact that people actually froze in place where they were. Those who had been directly around Becky Myers backed away so as to give her room to speak.

"Hello, little girl!" said Chip.

"And what's your name?" asked Flim.

"Becky Myers," she said with confidence. The two brothers each raised an eyebrow and looked at each other before turning back to Becky.

"Any relation to the mayor?" they said in unison.

"Yes!" shouted Olivia Myers, awkwardly shuffling through the crowd to stand at her daughter's side, although Becky made an irritable sidestep when she got there.

"You can't just cancel Halloween and replace it with your own holiday. Who do you think you are?"

"Rebecca!"

"Lovely daughter you have there, mayor," Flim teased.

"She must get her public speaking skills from you," mocked Chip. "But to answer your question, little girl, we are the Gonzo Brothers! Purveyors of all things which go bump in the night. We're entertainers, but we're businessmen as well, and a monopoly sounds like a lovely goal to strive towards, doesn't it?"

"But you can't just own Halloween! That's ridiculous."

"I agree," nodded Flim. "And how fortunate then that your town cancelled that wretched holiday for us. It was bad for business; we find it much more agreeable this way."

"You need to let that scarecrow go right now." To punctuate her demand, Becky took a dramatic step forward. There was something about the showmen's smiles which bore into her, though, and her wavering resolve pushed her a step back.

"We don't have to do anything, Miss Myers." Chip Gonzo closed the gap between them as he spoke. "We may be in Whisper Falls, but I assure you, we are playing on Gonzo territory now. However, I sense this isn't something you'll let go lightly."

"You can bet your stupid top hat on it, mister." Behind them, Flim let out a quick chortle, only to be silenced by a venomous look from his brother.

"Alright then," Chip said through a gritted smile. He straightened his back and held out his hands to address the whole crowd. "We'll play a game then, one anyone in Whisper Falls can play if they so choose!"

"Six keys," declared Flim, waving his hand like a window washer. Green mist took the shape of the promised items. "Six keys are hidden somewhere in this fine fair of ours."

"But," continued Chip. "Only three are necessary to free our dear Spirit. Two for the pillory, one for the chains. Bring them to us before midnight and he's yours. Fail, and expect to see Gonzo Day cards at your local pharmacy next September."

"Those are the only consequences?" asked Becky.

"There are consequences in everything, Rebecca," lamented Flim.

"Often greater and more numerous than you might initially anticipate," warned Chip.

"Where do we find these stupid keys?"

"In the rides and in the games, of course! If you want your keys, tokens must be consumed."

"Now enjoy, Whisper Falls, and have a happy Gonzo Day!" The two brothers levitated for a split second before bursting into that same green mist, which blended with the natural translucent fog of the evening and disappeared.

Mayor Myers watched her daughter run to the quickly dispersing crowd, petitioning anyone and everyone to help her and her friends find the keys. If there was any interest, they didn't show it. Some mumbled a quick decline, while others didn't even bother saying anything before walking away. She supposed this was to be expected; Becky wasn't the only one desperate to have some fun tonight.

"Okay, guys," she said to Avery and Joe. "It looks like we're on our own. We only get six chances, so maybe we better split up."

"Oh, joy," moaned Avery. "Going off alone in what is clearly a haunted carnival."

"I wouldn't say 'clearly' haunted," Joe laughed. "Just 'potentially' haunted. Our chances are way better with just 'potentially' haunted, right?"

"A scavenger hunt sounds fun," said Joe's father. "We'd be playing games and going on rides anyway, right? Might as well look for keys while we're at it."

"I can provide a police escort, I suppose." Officer Addams hitched up his belt theatrically, likening himself in his internal monologue to John Wayne. Avery lovingly thought he'd be lucky to get compared to Chief Wiggum.

"Great, more bodies!" Becky turned to her mom. "Not you, though."

"Excuse me, young lady?"

"There are only six keys. If you get your hands on enough of them, Halloween is over."

"Why are you so sure I don't want to help?" Olivia's eyes had gotten a little puffy, which made her look more like her daughter.

"You haven't for a year now, Mom. I don't expect you to start now." Her tone was dull, but her words still cut the mayor enough to make her cry. As Becky stormed off, Charlie turned to her.

"The kid has had a tough year," he said sympathetically.

"Yeah, no thanks to me."

"Hey, none of that now. I don't know what's going on here, exactly, but a little nighttime revelry might be good for your girl. Just give her time."

"Charlie," said the mayor, wiping her tears away and replacing her frown with steely resolve. "Get those damn keys, okay?"

Watching his superior stomp away angrily, Officer Addams couldn't help but mutter to himself, "like mother, like daughter, I guess."

It didn't take Becky long to reach her destination. She made sure to call dibs on the Ferris wheel when devising a gameplan, although she got no argument. Signs had informed her that the wheel was known as 'The Eye of Anubis,' and it stood like a misty silver eye overlooking the whole carnival.

The carny running it was a gaunt woman whose arms and chest were completely covered in tattoos. She winked at Becky as she took her tokens and helped her into her seat, and the girl couldn't help but blush as the ride jerked into motion. Going up was like floating into a cloud, with the haze that accentuated the wheel being thickest around the middle.

When she was fully immersed, there was a strange noise which Becky couldn't place at first. Shapes moved in the fog just outside her seat, and suddenly she could feel her heart beating in her chest. Joe and Avery said this place might be haunted, but clearly there was more to it than that. Who were the Gonzo Brothers that they could just chain the spirit of a holiday? What dangers were they capable of which she had gotten her friends involved in? What had she gotten herself into?

"Hey, pumpkin."

The voice came before a weight plopped down in her cabin. Accompanying it was a wind too cold even for this late in October, and Becky could see her breath. It was all she could focus on, her fear freezing her in place.

"This is pretty weird, isn't it? Sorry, I should have been better prepared." The bumbling way the voice spoke was enough to snap Becky out of it. There was something familiar about it, and she had to turn her head to confirm the gnawing suspicion.

"D-Dad?" she stuttered. "I... I don't—"

"Believe it, sweetheart. I guess I— oh, please don't start crying. If you cry, I'm going to cry. How about a hug for your old man?"

Becky leaned in to hug the ghost of her father. It wasn't like in the movies, where the living person just passed through like they were grasping smoke. To Becky, the sensation was more like touching two magnets together, an intangible force preventing them from fully connecting. The act was cold and unsatisfying; nothing like what a hug from her father should have been.

"How are you here?!"

"I think it's this wheel," said Leonard Myers, scratching his incorporeal head. "Acts as a kind of gate between this world and the next. These Gonzo jokers play hardball, I guess."

"But... why would the wheel show me you? You're not exactly scary, y'know."

“That’s the worst thing you can say to a ghost!” her father mocked.

“I’m serious, Dad.”

“Well, it’s because you're still a kid, kiddo— not that many dead people, yet, and not that many regrets. Which is how it should be. But the wheel can't break you with things you don't have.”

The noises in the mist suddenly became clearer to Becky. Screams and weeping blended together in a mournful melody, people forced to face those they had buried or said goodbye to, what they didn’t want to see and what they couldn’t bear to look at. Hearing all that pain made Becky sadder than she thought was possible.

“Careful, now,” said her dad. “You can’t help people sail the sea of misery if you’ve got a hole in your boat.”

“You sound like Avery’s dad,” Becky laughed, wiping away a tear.

“How’s ol’ Charlie doing? He a captain yet?”

“He’s not even a sergeant.”

“For the love of— okay, gotta focus. Ferris wheel rides aren’t that long, so we haven’t got much time.”

“Right!” said Becky, hiding the well of emotions she felt behind a determined façade. “I get straight As in school. Well, a few As, but the rest are Bs! Okay, one C, but geography is hard!”

“I was never good at geography,” Leonard smiled. One of the advantages to being translucent, he found, was that it was harder for people to notice when you're crying.

"I want to be a talk show host when I grow up. Or maybe a writer. I think I'm scared of bees but not wasps, which is weird because wasps are the more harmful ones. My favorite food is—"

"Hey, pumpkin?" her dad interrupted. "Your ride's almost over. I promise I want to hear all of this, and I might just hear it next time you're alone in the dark or talking to yourself in the cemetery. But I'd make the next one count, sweetie."

"I… I love you Dad. I miss you so much. Mom and I are fighting, and I don't know if it's ever going to get better, and I'm really scared."

"You and your mom will be okay," he told her, embracing his daughter with the strange magnet hug one more time. "I love you both so much, even if you've got a couple of thick skulls." It relieved Leonard Myers to no end that he could still make his daughter laugh when she was upset.

"I'll let you in on a secret, kiddo: you don't just magically figure stuff out when you grow up. Your mom is probably scared and confused too. Go easy on her, speak your mind, and forgive yourself and her for when one of you messes up. Or, y'know, I'll haunt the heck out of ya!"

"Dad," Becky groaned, praying the ride would last just a little longer. The cloud began to thin, and so too did the image of her father.

"Oh crap, I forgot to look for a key!"

"I'd scold you for language," said the disappearing apparition, "but I cuss like a damn sailor, too. They don't let us carry coins in the afterlife, but maybe you can put this in the swear jar." In his wispy hand was a brass key shaped like an ankh.

"How did you—?!"

"Grabbed it when we were at the very top. You're too easy to distract; that's why you liked my magic tricks so much." He went to hand the item to her, and it fell into her palm when he disappeared. The last Becky saw of him was his mouth forming the words 'I love you.'

Across the fairground, Joe Prince weighed the tokens in his hand carefully. An indecisive boy by nature, he had a hard time narrowing down his choices from the plethora of rides and games in the midway.

People often told Joe he overcomplicated things. He spent so much time weighing every detail that he never saw the straightforward answers in front of him. His dad had told him about Ockham's razor, the idea of cutting away unnecessary details until you had the simplest solution. So what details weren't unnecessary, then?

There were only six keys in the whole carnival, but dozens of attractions they could be hidden in. The Gonzo Brothers were gamesmen; they wouldn't make things easy, but it would still be solvable. He thought to what the pair had said before they disappeared, absentmindedly running his thumb over the tokens in his hand.

That's when it hit him.

"Gonzos!" he shouted, failing to consider there might be people around to find him odd. This was a recurring problem for Joe. "I've solved your riddle!"

Four glowing red eyes came into view down a dark alley, a space between a snack stand and the shooting gallery where bright carnival lights did not reach. They moved in perfect unison, like they belonged to some long-extinct apex predator out for blood. The light eventually illuminated their owners, brothers Chip and Flim Gonzo.

"A riddle?" questioned Chip. "What riddle are you privy to, Joe Prince?"

"You know my name?" His confidence suddenly felt less than total.

"Of course we do!" Flim tittered. "We're all friends here. Tell us what you found!"

"Your tokens!" he revealed, holding out his hand as if they were all the explanation he needed.

"Beautiful coins," Chip observed.

"Legal tender anywhere within our domain," added Flim.

"Beautiful coins... made of chocolate!" Joe peeled back the metal foil on one of the tokens, revealing slick milk chocolate underneath. "You said the tokens had to be consumed. Who talks like that unless they're giving a hint? I eat these and you fork over a key."

“What an interesting thought process,” said Flim. Chip said nothing, narrowing his eyes as the boy put coin after coin in his mouth.

“Ha, that’s all of them. Pay up!” Joe had a hand outstretched to receive his prize, but it quickly shot to his stomach, clutching it as an odd sensation gurgled within.

“Oh, Joseph,” scoffed Flim Gonzo. “Didn’t anyone ever teach you not to take candy from strangers?”

But,” Joe gagged. “You... said we were friends?”

“Grow up,” laughed Chip. “We’re carnival folk, the eternal strangers. And tokens are only to be consumed by our fair. You’ve created an imbalance in the Universe, one not easily rectified.”

Joe staggered away. His mouth became unbearably dry, like his throat was lined with the grittiest sandpaper. Heat blazed off his forehead, his body no doubt trying to purge whatever evil communion he had inside him. Water became his only priority. There was a lemonade cart down the midway, but his knees felt weak. He collapsed next to a post with a dirty hose attached to it. With fading hope, he turned the spout handle, and water actually trickled out. Like a suckling piglet, he began to drink the water.

The Gonzo Brothers were the only ones to witness what happened next; the carnival didn’t want anyone else to see. The post which held the hose began to splinter and crack, spitting out huge boards and poles. They connected around Joe, forming a new carnival booth. This occurrence unnerved Joe, but his only worry was quenching his thirst. When it felt for a second like he was satisfied, he tried to turn off the hose but found he couldn't. His arms wouldn't move at all; they had been swallowed by the walls of the booth.

Joe tried in vain to scream, but the jet of water prevented any sound from getting out. The hose was now on one side of the booth and his body was on the other. The water pressure became immense, and a pole ripped through Joe's back. The surface of every board in the booth began to ripple and change, taking on enticing colors. Soon Joe's eyes glazed over, and his roaring head was joined by seven others with their own water guns to douse them. Joe felt everything, constantly drowning but unable to die.

"Master of Tides," Flim read off the sign atop the now brightly lit booth. "A bit abstract, isn't it?"

"I think you're right," exhaled Chip. He waved his hand, and the words 'Water Gun Race' appeared beneath the original title. People were already flocking to play the game, and Joe wordlessly begged that they wouldn't.

"I really wish you wouldn't," said Charlie Addams some distance away. He had gotten separated from Avery while looking for an information booth. None appeared, and there were no security guards of any kind. Avery had run off, chasing what they claimed had been a lead but never elaborated on.

"Dad?" called a familiar voice. Charlie turned towards a building marked simply as 'House of

Mirrors.' "Dad?!" the voice called again from within, this time more urgently.

"Oh, cripes," sighed the cop. There was no one around the attraction, and Charlie wondered if it was even in operation. He poked his head inside and could hear sobbing, which to him sounded like his Avery was in trouble. "Damn carnival folk," he muttered under his breath before stepping inside.

The House of Mirrors was dark, so he switched on his flashlight. Suddenly dozens of shadow men appeared, his own silhouette reflected endlessly. Something about the way the mirrors caught the light didn't seem correct, but he had bigger concerns.

"Avery! You in here?"

"Might be," came a new voice, and Charlie turned so quick to face it he wound up slamming his head on a wall of glass.

"Dammit all!"

"Careful," the voice said pertly. "It's notoriously easy to get turned around in here. Have you lost someone, officer?"

"Yeah, my kid." He rubbed his forehead and looked around for another actual human being. "Who are you?"

"Can you describe your child, Officer Addams?"

"Uh, light brown hair? Kinda short? Jean vest, purple shirt. Denim pants. Wait, how did you—?"

"Are they a boy or a girl?"

"What?"

"Surely it can't be that difficult of a question." Something about the way they spoke was familiar but aggressive, almost predatorial.

"T-They don't..."

"Speak up, officer! Sound doesn't travel that well in here."

"They don't really go by either!" Charlie croaked.

"Oh," said the voice, sounding a little disappointed. "That's odd."

"Yeah, it's— wait, no! It's... it isn't weird."

"You agreed with me for a second, Officer Addams. Not entirely sure of your answer?"

"No..."

"No, you're not sure?"

"No, I *am* sure! Who the hell are you, anyway?" He waved his flashlight around trying to catch a glimpse. Even his own face was out of focus, save for the reflection immediately in front of him. He looked tired, older than he remembered. Just as he turned the flashlight away, he noticed something wrong. When he aimed it back at his reflection, he saw that it was smiling... when he wasn't.

"Boo!" shouted the reflection, banging its fist on the inside of the glass. Charlie yelped and nearly dropped his flashlight. The reflection laughed at him; even in the dark he could see it keeling over.

"What kind of trick—?"

"No trick, officer!" it explained. "No more than the one you play on yourself every day."

"My trick?"

"Have you considered you can't find 'Avery' because you don't know who that is?" Charlie took a step back at the accusation.

"They're my kid!"

"Are they? That's not what you named them when they were born."

"Yeah, they... didn't like that one. What business is it of yours?"

"I'm you, pal," the reflection chuckled. "Like it or not, I'm the genuine Charles."

"That doesn't make any sense," Charlie stammered. He looked around at his other reflections; none of them would meet his eye.

"Doesn't it?" the insidious reflection spat. "The you that sometimes gets things wrong? The you that still doesn't fully understand his child, even when they've explained it a dozen times?"

"Shut up..."

"The you that Avery is eventually going to get sick of and walk away from?"

"Shut up!"

"You can't shut me up, Charles."

"I can sure as hell try." Charlie drew his gun and aimed it at his reflection.

“You’re not going to shoot me, officer.”

“Wanna bet?”

“You’re not going to shoot me because you’re a coward, Charles. Just an old dinosaur who can’t make sergeant, can’t fix his diet to save his life, and can’t stop his kid from hating him!”

Charlie fired the gun. The sound was deafening as it echoed around the room. The mirror cracked, but didn’t shatter. His reflection was wounded on the right shoulder. Mercury spilled out from it in place of blood. A blinding pain shot through Charlie’s left shoulder, but as far as he could tell, there was no actual injury. He let loose five more shots, breaking apart the mirror and knocking the creature inside on its back.

He stepped over its body, a mangled and writhing thing which barely resembled him anymore. The more playful part of his nature compelled him to say a witty one-liner like a movie star would, but his whole body was in agony, and this thing didn’t deserve it anyway. After firing one more shot, he saw something glint in the creature’s hand, a chrome key which he happily snatched.

“Dad!” the real Avery shouted at him as he made his way out of the House of Mirrors. He walked as if he had just gotten into a fight with the Incredible Hulk, and looked as if he had bet money on himself. “Dad, say something.”

“You know I love you, right?” Charlie said after collapsing to his knees and putting his arms around Avery’s shoulders.

"Uh, yeah? Dad, what are you doing?"

"Just listen," he blubbered. "I know I get stuff wrong a lot, and I'm confused by just about everything. But I'm so proud of the person you are, and the person you're becoming. You don't ever need to do anything or be anything to have my approval, okay? Not a damn thing."

Avery was silent for a moment before returning their father's hug. "I know you get stuff wrong, Dad. You're old, these things happen." Charlie let out a laugh, which made Avery smile. "I'm still figuring stuff out too, and I wouldn't be able to do that if I didn't have your support. You care enough to learn from your mistakes, and I appreciate that."

"So… we're okay?" he asked, pulling away and getting to his feet.

"Always. Now let's go find Becky."

A small crowd had gathered around the platform which held Spirit O'Halloween. Despite their earlier apathy, Whisper Falls was invested in the holiday's fate, and they hoped the mayor's daughter could pull through.

"Avery!" she called. "Did you get them?"

"Eyup," said Avery, proudly displaying a white key covered in polka-dots. "I had to fight some really weird clowns to get it, but they weren't that tough."

"You got one too, Mr. Addams?"

"Yeah, I… had to do a little self-reflection, but I got it." He handed her the chrome key and looked around for her mother.

"Then that's three!" Becky cheered.

"Good evening, Whisper Falls!" bellowed Flim Gonzo from atop the platform. "Have we delivered on all we promised?" Cacophonous applause erupted from the crowd.

"You're welcome!" shouted Chip. "It's less than ten minutes until midnight, so we'd like to invite Becky Myers and all her little friends to come up here and tell us how they did tonight!"

The crowd clapped as the three ascended the rickety staircase. Becky looked to Spirit, who was as motionless as ever. The light inside his pumpkin head seemed too dim, nearly extinguished.

"Were you successful, Miss Myers?" Flim asked. The trio each held up their prizes, and the brothers seemed giddy for someone who had just been foiled.

"Well done!" Chip commended them. "All that's left then is to free your holiday friend." Becky looked out into the crowd anxiously. "Is there something wrong, Rebecca?"

"It's just... I thought my mom would be here to see this. And where are Joe and his dad?"

"Oh, we have them."

"What?!"

"We told you there were consequences," snickered Flim. "You play, you pay. Mr. Prince the elder tried to grab a prize from our claw machine, but the machine wound up grabbing him instead. Mr. Prince the younger, meanwhile, thought he could outsmart us, but we drowned those aspirations swiftly and efficiently."

"And your mother," continued Chip. "We had a lovely chat with her not half an hour ago, and afterwards sent her off towards a quaint little fishing game with a promise there was a key there. There was more in those depths than she bargained for, though, and I'm afraid your mother was pulled under."

"No!" Becky shouted.

"Hold it, freakshow," declared Charlie Addams, stepping forward and aiming his gun directly at the brothers, earning a gasp from the crowd. "I've just about had it with this spooky scary shit."

"Officer," said Chip Gonzo.

"Are you familiar with the phrase 'this will hurt me more than it will hurt you'?" asked Flim.

"Yeah?"

"Well, I assure you, firing your weapon right now would hurt you more than it will hurt us."

"Bring them back!" interjected Becky. "You bring all three of them back now!"

"We could," admitted Chip.

"But we won't," laughed Flim. "Not for free."

"What do you want for them, then?"

The brothers shared a knowing look. "Oh, not much," Chip said slyly.

"Just one of your keys!" squeaked Flim. "Specifically your key, Rebecca. Give us that and we return your lost property, simple as that."

"But..." Becky considered, eyes on the key in her hand. "We only have three?"

"It's almost as if that's the point," Chip spat. "Not every choice is apple juice or OJ, child. Sometimes it's life or death, business or pleasure. Better make your choice quickly. It's nearly midnight."

Becky looked from the Gonzos to Avery and Mr. Addams, both of whom looked mortified for her. The crowd was even less helpful, blankly waiting for things to play out. She almost broke down until she caught a glimpse of the Ferris wheel off in the distance.

"Have the key," she said, holding it out to the Gonzos. Flim snatched it up quickly, and the pair watched the brass melt in his clutch.

Three new bodies appeared on the platform, and the crowd gasped again. Joe's father was on his back, holding an old-fashioned cymbal monkey toy. He seemed to notice it for the first time and threw it away in horror. Assured that it couldn't hurt him, he ran to his son, who was coughing up water and being tended to by Avery.

"Mom!" cried Becky. The mayor looked as if she had been dunked in a bog, her whole body dripping with foul, green water, moss and mud covering her from head to toe. Becky hugged her in spite of it. "I'm so glad you're okay! I don't care about Halloween, alright? It's over anyway, we lost."

"I don't know about that," whispered the mayor, slipping something into Becky's hand.

"What do you have there?" demanded Chip.

Becky understood immediately. She nodded at Avery, who grabbed the key from their father and joined her in running towards the pillory. The polka-dot and mirror keys fit the locks around the scarecrow's arms, and the key from Becky's mother, a rusty green one, unlocked the black chains.

"No!" barked Flim. "You lost, so that means no more Halloween!" He loped towards the pillory but was immediately thrown across the platform into his brother.

Becky couldn't explain what had happened. She didn't see the scarecrow move, but nevertheless it stood as if it had gotten out of its restraints. It was completely still, save for the raging candle flame in its head. Chip and Flim Gonzo, who had toppled over one another, looked at the immobile Spirit and screamed in terror.

A fierce wind picked up, whipping circus garbage all about. It was the kind of wind which preceded a terrible rainstorm, but the night sky was clear. Becky was nearly blown off the platform, but Avery caught her by the arm. Her mother hugged her to keep her steady.

"What now?" Olivia asked her daughter. A sound like a whipcrack alerted them to the big top, which was becoming unlatched one rope at a time.

"I think now we run!" Becky shouted over the accelerating air currents.

"Ok, people; show's over!" Charlie shouted to the crowd, who were already beginning to panic and scatter. "Back to your cars, step lively! You don't have to go home, but I wouldn't recommend staying here!"

A snack stand flew into the sky, and there was a powerful creak from the Eye of Anubis, suggesting it wasn't far behind. Owen took his son into his arms. Charlie and Avery helped him off the platform, which was rocking back and forth. Becky took one last look at the eight-foot-tall scarecrow, seeing if it would take any other action against its captors, but the brothers had disappeared; one last showman's trick. The wind blew on just the same, finally sending the big top high into the sky.

"Time to go, kiddo," Olivia said, grabbing Becky by the hand.

The young Myers girl would swear to Avery and Joe later that Spirit had winked at her before being blown away in its own wind, but when they asked her for details, she found she couldn't conjure them; the moment was hers alone. The platform crumbled and was sucked up into the sky just as both mayor and daughter made it off the last step. The six were some of the last to make it out, encouraging stragglers to get a move on.

The wind was tamer outside the fairgrounds, and the citizens of Whisper Falls safely made their egress by foot or by car. Avery went with Becky and her mom, Joe and Owen getting into the back of Charlie's squad car. In the mayor's sedan, Becky and Avery watched the rest of the carnival get pulled skyward. The cyclone flew off, the circus lights still lit briefly enough to take the shape of a happy jack-o'-lantern before dispersing among the stars.

Becky smiled to herself as a feeling came over her, one she couldn't quite name. It was a kind of hope, but not hope in the general sense. It was the kind of hope a child felt in its mother's arms, the kind a cynic experienced after accepting a miracle. There were no decorations up, but the trees were still orange and the sky was still black. No costumes had been bought, no candy had been sold, but despite it all, Becky Myers smiled because today was Halloween.

The Teratier

"Adversity makes men, and prosperity makes monsters." -Victor Hugo

The difference between fifteen and eighteen is a relatively small number, but to a teenager, it's astronomical. Mike Mychenko was only eighteen years old, but in the eyes of Griffin and his friends, those three years he had on them may as well have made him a god. None of them ever stopped to question why a kid in twelfth grade would want to hang out with lowly tenth-graders like them. They didn't want to acknowledge that Mike wasn't nearly as cool as they made him out to be; he was an outcast from his peers, a clear representation of how they each felt about themselves, whether or not it was actually true. Their group related to Mike, looked up to him. When you're fifteen, you'd follow someone like that to Hell and back.

The group always had five members, apart from in the very beginning when they were still recruiting. There was Griffin, described by anyone but himself as the heart of the group. Still finding himself, he was a practicing coward unless the safety or honor of one of his friends was in jeopardy. His best friend was Athena, who had all the personality quirks of a girl who went through middle school with an unusual first name. True to her namesake, though, she was remarkably clever and unshakable in her confidence in her abilities. Athena had nothing to prove to anybody.

Olivia was the only goth of the group, there because she had been rejected by the other goths for being too soft and comparatively upbeat. This was, of course, hilarious to her friends, who found her gloomy disposition, while vexing on the odd occasion, generally quite droll. They never hesitated attempting to lift her spirits should she actually be depressed, and they were never less than accepting of her the rest of the time.

Rounding out the younger members was Jonah, a human-shaped accumulation of sweat, random useless facts, and undiagnosed ADHD. Always interrupting teachers with questions and throwing himself into projects he had no business being in, Jonah was the kind of guy people were sure would go on to either be homeless or a millionaire; anything in between didn't seem right. On paper, Jonah shouldn't have fit in with the others at all, being more interested in cars or track and field. But he stuck around because he found the 'normal' students to be boring, and he was amicable to learning about the strange movies and anime his friends were into.

And then there was Mike, their fearless leader. The group voted on everything as a democracy, but it was Mike who initiated the vote. In the winter, they mostly played video games, only venturing out into the frozen oblivion of Whisper Falls once or twice to trim a tree, eat some festive cookies, or watch holiday specials nearly older than half the group combined. In spring, they were urban explorers, finding secret corners of their hometown revealed by the thawing snow and enabled by a sudden enthusiasm for going outside. In the summer, they watched movies; whether in theaters or in basements, it didn't matter.

But autumn was special. September was dominated in the first week by the need to hold on to summer, and the rest by back-to-school hullabaloo, so they made up for it in October. One day every week, going by whichever day that Halloween would fall on that year, they told scary stories. While each of their seasonal traditions held monopolies on different corners of their hearts, there was something unique about this one. They had each been collectively united by the terror they had inspired in one another.

And this year was going to be extra special. It had to be. An arbitrary zoning decision by the city council had placed all of them, along with approximately two hundred other students, into different school districts, meaning they would no longer be classmates in the new year. To make matters worse, Mike's family was moving away over Christmas break. Though he was technically a legal adult, he had nothing in the way of finances, and his parents were unwilling to pay for an apartment, meaning he had no choice but to go with them. Seeing the melancholic air that had befallen the group after this two-pronged attack on their friendship, Mike promised a Halloween they wouldn't forget.

They made a point to go trick-or-treating no matter what. "Until we're adults, we're kids," Mike would say. "And kids get to ask people for free candy on October 31st. The social contract says it's okay!"

"Feels like the only time the social contract has ever done anything for us," Athena observed.

"So we'd be rude to refuse such a gift!" Jonah said emphatically.

They would meet at six o'clock at the school, just before sundown. Normally the building would be inaccessible to them, but Olivia's uncle taught math and social studies and allowed them use of his classroom, provided they weren't longer than an hour, and didn't get up to, in his words, 'naughty satanic hooey.' It was tradition that Mike be the one to orate his story on Halloween, since it was unanimous that his stories were always the best. Once he was done, if they all weren't terrified beyond reason, they would go out to collect their sweets.

In preparation for the night, Mike told everyone a month in advance that he wanted them to pick costumes that adhered to a theme: made-monsters. It was a peculiar request, one that Mike refused to elaborate on, but it was a challenge which captured their inspiration. And as a credit to their collective imagination, no two costumes in the group were the same.

Griffin had taken the easy, obvious route, letting himself procrastinate until the eleventh hour. He came dressed as Frankenstein's monster, a decision which earned him razzing from every one of his friends in one form or another. Athena wore spider legs on her back, and a white doily hung over her face which served the role of a veil of webs.

"I'm Arachne," she announced. "The original Athena turned her into a spider for boasting, and all modern spiders are her descendants."

"Didn't Athena also turn Medusa into a monster?" asked Griffin.

"Yeah, and?"

"I'm just saying, Medusa would have worked too, and been more recognizable."

"I didn't dress up as Arachne to be recognizable," said Athena, mildly offended. "I went with Arachne because she's a cool spider lady, whose only crime was being confident in herself, and she gave birth to one of the most badass species on the planet. Medusa is overdone, as far as I'm concerned."

Jonah's costume earned a laugh, being a head-to-toe dinosaur get-up which looked cumbersome to move in. He explained it was meant to be Godzilla, the kaiju created by atomic radiation, but the best he could find was a used mascot suit. Far more impressive was Olivia's costume, a completely handmade Edward Scissorhands ensemble. The blades that made up the titular scissors were paper mâché and worn on top of her real hands in a seamless illusion, allowing her to still make use of her fingers should she need them. When she announced she had spent nearly ninety minutes getting her makeup just right, her friends applauded her.

"I'm so proud of all of you," said Mike, who was waiting for them inside. He wore a long, gray coat one might expect to see on a mad scientist, and thick rubber gloves which did not look comfortable or practical. His entire face was painted to look like a character from a black and white movie, but one whose skeleton was being emphasized under their skin.

"Well, Mike," said Athena. "If your plan was to have us all marvel at your costume, you've failed miserably; none of us have any idea who you are."

"I'm Dynamo Dan," Mike replied. "From the 1941 film *Man-Made Monster*, the story of a sideshow worker who can't be harmed by electricity, but after being experimented on by a mad scientist, he becomes a monster hungry for energy."

"Leave it to Mike to pick a costume from a movie that hasn't been seen by anyone born in the last thirty years," laughed Jonah.

"It's an unappreciated masterpiece!"

"I think it's cool..." Olivia said sheepishly.

"So what's the game, Mike?" smiled Griffin, feeding off the positive energy in the room the same way Dynamo Dan fed off the life force of his victims. "You've given us a clear theme, but why?"

"Ah, because it pertains to tonight's story," Mike said before laughing maniacally, producing a black candle from inside one of his gloves. "Athena, could you please light the candle? I would, but," and he gestured to the gloves on his hands. "Jonah, hit the lights?" Godzilla took a crumpled water bottle he had been drinking from and threw it at the dim fluorescent lights on the ceiling.

"You're hilarious," Athena said sarcastically as she fought to ignite her zippo. Once the candle was burning, Olivia ran over to the light switch and shrouded them all in partial darkness.

"Take a seat, friends," Mike instructed stoically, adding a cryptic gravitas to his tone that he always used before storytelling. "But remember, once you've joined the circle, it cannot be broken for anything."

Griffin was the first to sit in one of the chairs Mike had arranged around a single desk in the middle of the room, where the lit black candle now stood. The others followed suit one by one, and when everyone was seated and had stopped their typical fidgeting, Mike took a breath and began.

"You've all entered this circle having borrowed the guise of a made-monster, those who were created by others. Tonight's story is not about the monsters, but those who make them. One monster-maker in particular, actually; a local celebrity. A teratier."

"A what?" Jonah blurted out, his frank confusion doing little to maintain the atmosphere Mike had been cultivating.

"There's no way you didn't make that word up," Athena derided.

"Guys, don't interrupt!" hissed Olivia.

"I'm guessing from the context that it means someone who makes monsters," posited Griffin. The other sophomores turned to him, all with thoughts quick to deride the obvious statement, but stopping themselves when they realized they hadn't thought of it first. "But why that word? Where does it come from?"

"Regardless of whether or not I coined the term," Mike smirked, "I envision it will catch on sooner or later. It comes from the Greek 'terato-', meaning—"

"Monster or monstrous," Athena interrupted. "Which tells me the '-ier' is meant to signify someone's job, like courier, or financier."

"Or chocolatier," Jonah said dreamily. "Man, we're going to get so much candy tonight."

"Guys!" went Olivia again. "Let Mike finish the story."

“Thank you, Edward,” said Mike, winking at Olivia and making her blush, evident from the way she shifted bashfully in her seat if not through her makeup. “Now where was I? Ah, yes. Each of your costumes calls to mind a particular teratier from fiction, each one with different motives and means for creating their monsters. But the one I bring your attention to tonight is no work of fiction, but a real man, one who was born and raised right here in Whisper Falls. The sights that shaped his young mind were the same that we see every day. Ladies and gentleman, this is the twisted tale of Doctor Carver.

“Full name Elliot Madison Carver, born sometime in the early fifties. His exact date of birth is unknown, because the original hospital records were destroyed. This town tried to erase him entirely because of his crimes, but obviously that was impossible. There are still old folks around here who remember him, or remember the family, at least. The library has whole boxes of microfiche that they forgot to redact, waiting to be pieced together into the portrait of an ordinary family, and their ordinary little boy who grew up to become the most notorious and savage killer this town has ever produced, and one of the most unique evils this country has ever seen.”

“What did he do?” Griffin whispered. He was so caught up in the story that he didn't realize at first that he was saying it out loud. In fear of being scolded, he glanced at Olivia, but she was hanging onto Mike's every word too; they all were.

“Well, my friends,” Mike said before a dramatic pause. “He did a lot.

"Doctor Carver was a brilliant surgeon and biologist. Any accolades or renown he may have had in his old life, though, were blotted out by the shadow of his misdeeds. Whatever college or university had given him a degree threw out their paperwork faster than the hospital did. While his credentials went up in smoke, that did little to stop the world from still calling him 'doctor.'

"Carver was head-hunted by a government firm shortly after finishing his education, specifically for something known as Project Shelley. You see, the Vietnam War had scared the bejesus out of the west. Everyone was thinking about what the next conflict was going to be, and how soldiers would fare in it. The purpose of Project Shelley was to find the limits of what humans could withstand— and push past those limits. Science could tell them how to make a more resilient soldier, a stronger soldier, a better soldier."

"We can rebuild him, we have the technology," muttered Jonah, doing his best impression of the intro to *The Six Million Dollar Man*. Everyone laughed, although they did so while throwing condemning looks his way.

"It didn't take long for Carver to be made one of the top authorities within Project Shelley," Mike continued. "A lot of his contemporaries walked away after seeing what was expected of them, meaning the government was desperate for someone exactly like Carver: a prodigy with no moral compass. They were more than happy to keep giving him greater and greater power."

“Too much power,” assessed Athena. “That’s typical.”

“Exactly right, my adept arachnid. With that much authority under his belt, Carver essentially had carte blanche to do whatever he liked with Shelley’s resources. He set up private labs all across the country, but Carver was a master at fixing paperwork. When orders to create one lab were submitted, they’d quickly be withdrawn or changed to a secondary location, but thanks to greased palms and general bureaucratic oversight, those first locations would be set up anyway, known only to Carver and the select few staff that worked there who were sworn to secrecy, assuming it was just part of their job.

“It took almost two years for anyone to notice, at least in a way that could actually be detrimental to Carver. You see, while Project Shelley kept hitting dead ends and making strides at a glacial pace, artificially manipulated by the madman running it, the real progress was being made in the shadows.

“Doctor Carver was a scientist, yes, but what few people understood was that he was also an artist. Project Shelley had given the doctor means to test his thesis, not the one he had written in school, but the thing which was the basis for his life’s work. The belief was simple: you could alter a person’s body virtually any way you wanted, as long as you didn’t need the subject to remain sane.

“It’s unclear exactly how many there were, but at least a couple dozen people were experimented on by Carver personally, turning them into his... art projects. Mercilessly. If you saw any of them now, you'd be hard-pressed to say they were human. Limbs were added and removed, flesh was torn, blood was drained, viscera—"

"Breaks!" Olivia said suddenly. The phrase was a kind of inside joke for the group, but one they all took seriously. It had begun not long after Mike had gotten his driver's license, the only one among them old enough to do so. No one remembered who said it first, but whenever he took a turn too sharply or allowed the car to exceed the speed limit in a residential area, one of the others would shout 'breaks!', and it had become their general codeword for 'something's wrong' or 'I'm not okay.'

"You alright, Scissorhands?" Mike asked attentively.

"Yeah, I'm good, just..." said Olivia before taking a few decisive breaths. "Maybe not so graphic, okay?"

"You got it. Now where was I? Oh yeah, the monsters. So excessive surgery and operations on a person gradually burns them out. Their bodies need time to recover from the excessive physical trauma, and the human mind can only take so much pain before something breaks in there. But Carver would overhaul them from top to bottom, replacing or improving anything which didn't stand up to his methods. Even the brain would be spared, thanks to the right combination of chemicals. Those whose minds weren't completely lost by the procedure would soon go mad after seeing and feeling what was done to them."

"You mentioned two years," Athena pointed out. "What happened after that?"

"Well, the power afforded to Carver allowed him to be virtually undetectable; his superiors rarely interacted with him outside of phone calls, and his subordinates were kept on a need-to-know basis regarding his activities and whereabouts. So, when he got word that he was being investigated, he began to slink back into the shadows, bouncing around from place to place."

"That's a good word, 'slink,'" Jonah mused. "More people need to slink."

"It wasn't until he made it back home that he was caught. And it wasn't the elite squad of government operatives that were hot on his trail who caught him. Even on the run, he was keeping up his work. His art was a compulsion at this point, an addiction. Maybe it was because he experimented on himself too. Not as drastically as his subjects, just little improvements here and there. So people around here went missing just before Halloween, including the nephew of a local cop. He was only a little older than us. The cop went on a manhunt, looking for the sicko who grabbed him. Carver was found eventually, and the cop's nephew hadn't been turned yet.

"But the others had. And the cop... well, he put them out of their misery, but not without considerable effort. Whatever Carver's process was, it made the subject nearly impossible to kill. Carver himself was half alive after the fight, and the cop brought him in. Locked him up right there in the local jail."

"The one on the corner of Main and Sanderson?" asked Griffin.

"The very same. Once all the hard work was actually done, those government agents swooped in and demanded Carver be released into their custody. While the cops and G-men argued over procedure, Carver seemed oddly... calm. Happy, even, like being captured was only a minor setback. The cop was the first one to notice this, but he couldn't get the others to listen in time. You see, Carver had way more of his creations lying around than anyone realized. And they didn't take too kindly to their boss being in danger.

"Monsters descended on the police station, and there was a bloodbath that Halloween night. The details get fuzzy afterwards, but one of the government guys must have called for backup, because Carver was ultimately taken into custody, the real secure kind, with pools of blood and dozens of bodies in his wake."

"What happened next?" asked Athena. "Something that big I'd imagine would have made the national news, but I've also never heard of Carver until tonight."

"There was some coverage, sure," said Mike, producing a large manilla envelope from his bag and throwing it on the desk between them. "This town wouldn't have worked so hard to erase his legacy if they hadn't at least found out what he did. But at some point, after a week or two, people just... stopped talking about it. Government censorship definitely played a part, although how big of a part is hard to say. But I don't know, maybe with something that horrific, it's easy to shut people up because they can't stand dwelling on it anyway. Like a scar you don't like looking at."

Olivia shifted uncomfortably in her seat, and when she saw people had noticed, she grabbed the manilla envelope and opened it. "So, w-what's in here?" she stuttered.

"That's everything I was able to find on Carver," Mike sighed, decompressing as his story neared its end. "Go ahead, look inside. It's mostly newspaper clippings and photocopies. There's a local conspiracy nutjob who helped me with a lot of it." Olivia did as she was told, dumping the folder's contents onto the desk, which were followed by a handheld tape recorder that landed with a small thud.

"What's this, then?"

"Oh, just an audio recording of me interviewing Langdon Coombs, otherwise known as the nephew of that cop who caught Carver."

"He's still alive?" Griffin asked in disbelief.

"Yup, one of the only survivors of that night. I found him in a long-term care facility on the outskirts of town. Pretty normal guy, although he has good days and bad ones. Turns out, he's done his fair share of research on Carver too."

"Ha, nerd!" belted Jonah.

"Jonah, we're all nerds here," Athena pointed out.

"Exactly, it takes one to know one."

"He had some interesting things to say," Mike continued. "Chief among them being that no one knows where Carver is."

"What?!" shouted Griffin and Jonah, nearly in unison.

"Yeah," laughed the storyteller. "Coombs and the local conspiracy nut are friends; how I found him. A few years ago, he tried to find Carver. He was sure he'd never be able to get close to him, but just knowing that monster from his past was safely locked up or dead would give him closure, y'know? He found other people who were interested in Carver, and they all told him the same thing: Carver is a ghost. Figuratively speaking, of course, but it could very well be literal for all they knew. No records anywhere, no government employees willing to speak the truth."

"Someone must have some idea," Athena objected.

"Plenty of theories. Some say they incinerated him, sealed his ashes in a box and dropped it in the Mariana Trench. Others think he's still working for the government, but with a much shorter leash."

"What do you think, Mike?" Olivia asked.

"My money's on a secure government black site. Threw him in the deepest, darkest hole they could find in case they ever need him again, but they're too afraid to actually use him."

"That might be the scariest option," said Griffin ominously.

"Explain," ordered Athena.

"Well, if that's the case, how long until he breaks out?"

The group sat in quiet contemplation on Griffin's words. Though no one was speaking, everyone agreed that he improved Mike's story with such a chilling notion, effectively giving him the win for the season. A lesser friend would have resented Griffin for snatching away victory with his own contribution, but Mike was just proud. Said victory never came with anything more than mere bragging rights, although winners were always slipped a little extra candy by everyone else when they went out trick-or-treating at last. Getting impatient for that time to begin, Jonah broke the silence with fervor.

"Alright, you monsters!" he shouted, causing everyone to jump in their seats and Olivia to let out a quick shriek. "We're losing moonlight! I say it's time we make our way through stygian night in search of treats! Who's with me?"

"Here, here!" Mike cheered.

"Here, here!" echoed the other three.

The group filed out of the room one by one. Griffin was last, feeling it was polite to let his friends take the lead. He started to follow them, but abruptly double-backed when he realized no one had blown out the candle. Griffin would remember that choice for years to come.

From one perspective, it was the most mundane action in the world, a bit of common sense by a responsible adolescent with basic knowledge of fire safety. But as Griffin enveloped the room in darkness once more, he couldn't help but feel a sense of foreboding. He was having a great time with his friends, and they would continue to have a great time as they prowled the neighborhood looking for candy and getting asked at least a dozen times if they thought they were getting a little old for trick-or-treating. But in that moment, it was the way the sudden blackness told him things were different now that Griffin would never forget.

The memory would come back to him ten years later, when another darkness found him. This one was different. It was cold and wet, filled with screams and the scent of meat that had gone bad. Griffin was exhausted. His arm was bleeding, and his shoes were soaking wet from traipsing through ankle-deep water.

"BRAHUK-KUH!" cried an inhuman thing from the darkness.

His mind was working in overdrive trying to keep him out of harm's way, but he was exhausted and agitated, and scared out of his wits. The best his subconscious could do was to take him back to how this whole mess had started, desperately searching for a detail he might have missed.

It began with a phone call. It was Athena, a girl he hadn't seen in over five years, or thought about in almost that long. But it was nice to hear her voice; it took him back to a simpler time, when he had direction in his life and no student loans. She said she was calling because she had just heard from their old pal Mike Mychenko for the first time in ages. He wanted to get their old crew back together, just for one night on Halloween in Whisper Falls like old times.

And Griffin had wanted to say no. The absence of purpose in his life was exhausting, and going out and doing things wasn't something exhausted people rushed into eagerly. However, that also meant he had nothing going on that could serve as an adequate excuse not to. It might be nice, he told himself, reconnecting with his past. The holiday was also only a week away, and home was only twenty minutes away by car, so he simply asked Athena for the exact time and place.

The answer to the latter was Jill's Place, a pub on the nicer side of town. Griffin arrived first, fashionably early to quell any anxiety about being late, or more specifically about being judged for being late. He sat alone in a booth for ten agonizing minutes, wondering if no one else was coming, or if he had somehow been pranked. But then Athena appeared before him, a little more tired in the face but otherwise the same girl he had gone to high school with. Her shoulder-length brown hair was now a short indigo faux hawk with the back of her head buzzed, and she wore a fashionable leather jacket that was so well-suited to her style that it may as well have been attached to her body.

Griffin stood up to greet her, and they did the awkward song and dance of not being sure to shake hands or hug. Once they were both seated, they made awkward small talk about the drive over and how their hometown had or hadn't changed in recent years, until Jonah arrived a few minutes later.

"Okay, whose intervention is it?" he joked. "And if it's mine, you gotta let me know now, because I'll want to have a drink first."

The three of them shared a laugh, and that put Griffin at ease, as did the fact that Jonah looked exactly like Griffin expected him to: exactly the same, just with a little more of a gut and a little less of a hairline. The next person to show up, though...

"Oh good, you found each other."

Mike Mychenko did not look well. It seemed as if a light breeze could blow him over, he was so malnourished. Stubble clung to his face like barnacles on the hull of an untended ocean vessel, and dark bags sat starkly under his eyes like they'd been hung from a rope attached to his eyebrows for gallows. He wore the same brown trench coat they had bought for him as a going-away present, now ten years older and in a ratty state of disrepair.

"Mike!" Griffin said, unsure of what other greeting would be appropriate.

"You look..." Athena began.

"Horrible," Jonah said playfully. "My god, man. I thought *I* let myself go."

"Jonah!" Griffin and Athena scolded Jonah in unison, the way they had dozens of instances when they were teenagers. Things really were like old times.

"What?" Jonah laughed. "I'm just making an observation. At least let me offer to buy the man a burger."

"That actually does sound good..." said Mike.

They ordered food and drinks while their former leader explained his shabby appearance. For the past four years, Mike had been living in his car. It wasn't economic or personal turmoil which had led to that decision, but a pre-emptive move. The neighborhood he had lived in was gentrifying fast, and he fully expected rising rent to drive him and lots of others out before long.

"It's not so bad," Mike said between bites of his hamburger. "Getting started while I still had money in the bank helped a lot, let me make mistakes without completely ruining things. I traded rent payments for gas money I was going to be spending anyway, and I work as a courier, so my car payments and upkeep are business expenses."

"You really have it all figured out," Athena smiled.

"Yeah, and a lot of people do what I do. They share tips online. I don't own a computer, but I'm never far away from a public library. Enough about me, though. What's everyone else been up to?"

"I'm a teaching assistant at Kroy University," said Athena. "Media Studies. It isn't so bad, but man, I just know my students hate my guts. I hated the TA my first year, and I'm an even harder marker than they were."

"The wrath of Athena strikes again," chuckled Jonah.

"Then what have you been doing, wise guy?"

"I've got my own auto business just a couple towns over. Well, I'm the co-owner, but the owner is my father-in-law, and he's retiring in a few years."

"Oh, you're married?" asked Mike.

"Yeah, just this past summer. And... I'm a dad."

Everyone stopped eating.

"You're kidding," said Griffin, face caught between a smile and pure doubt.

"What poor woman did you make a baby with?" Athena teased.

"No one," Jonah laughed, getting a little red. "The kid's hers from a previous relationship. I wasn't sure about him at first, but I was always sure I was crazy about her, and the kid needed a dad. So... here we are."

"Wow," Mike sighed. "How does it feel?"

"Honestly? Terrifying. I've never had to take care of something smaller than myself before. Heck, I couldn't even keep pet goldfish alive when I was a kid. Now there's this human being that gives me a heart attack every time he runs ahead of me at the park or the mall. It's surreal."

"What about you, Griff?" Athena asked.

"Oh, I..." Griffin stammered. He wasn't sure how much he wanted to elaborate. Then again, how could he elaborate on nothing? He was between jobs, and he had no significant other or family apart from his folks, although they had moved south not long after he had graduated. It wasn't like his old friends were movie stars or astronauts, but they were each doing something with their lives, not sitting at home watching reruns of *Star Trek* and *The Twilight Zone* because they could only afford basic cable.

"You good, man?" Jonah inquired.

"Yeah, just... wait, aren't we missing someone? Where's Olivia?"

"Oh my gosh, I was so caught up in everyone's stories!" Athena chided herself.

"Thank goodness," Jonah sighed in relief. "I thought everyone knew something I didn't."

They turned to Mike. "I reached out to her, same as you guys," he explained, not making eye-contact with anyone. "I expected her to be here, all five of us back together, but alas."

"Anyone heard from her over the years?" asked Griffin.

"We got coffee once during my first year at Kroy," said Athena. "She seemed... I dunno, troubled? I can't really put my finger on it. We didn't keep in touch, as much as I wanted to."

"Anyway," Mike declared. "I didn't invite you lot back here without a plan. I have a surprise— a two-part surprise, in fact."

"Oh, boy!" Jonah squeed.

"This isn't going to be anything weird, is it?" bemoaned Griffin.

"Maybe a little," snickered Mike. "But I promise you, it's worth it. Come on, I've gotta drive you to part one."

He led them outside to a black Chevy Z24 with mismatched hubcaps and a dent in the passenger side door. Before they could enter, Mike held up a hand and gestured them towards the trunk, which popped open to reveal three Halloween costumes.

"Shut up," Athena gasped in joy.

"No way," Jonah exclaimed. "You got us our old costumes?"

"Obviously they're not exactly the same," said Mike, opening his trench coat to reveal a second coat underneath, this one a familiar grayscale color. "Just what the local Shopper Mart could provide, but I figured we could try some trick-or-treating dressed as the same characters we were on our last Halloween together."

"At our age?" Athena scoffed. "Aren't we a little old for that? It would be like the bizarro version of kids getting on each other's shoulders to pretend they're adults."

"What are we, the Little Rascals?" Griffin laughed.

"I guess technically that would make us the *Big* Rascals," said Jonah, and the whole group erupted with laughter.

Despite the ridiculousness of the idea, all of them happily donned their costumes and got in Mike's car. They saw it as embracing the madness, to a certain extent, though there weren't many whose doors they knocked on that readily embraced it with them. A handful of suburbanites gave them handfuls of candy, either out of pity or festive bemusement, but the majority of Whisper Falls they visited simply told them to get lost or take a hike. With Mike's car, they hit several neighborhoods in quick succession. The twin advantages of adulthood, long legs and driver's licenses, made trick-or-treating easier than it ever had been as kids, so even their paltry spoils turned into a horde of potential cavities before long.

"We gotta bring this back for adults," said Jonah, slurping up a piece of licorice like spaghetti. "We can start a movement."

"It's funny," said Griffin. "We used to have to sort through our stuff for Olivia. Remember her peanut allergy?"

"Oh yeah," Athena said. "She was always really paranoid about it."

Griffin savored a chocolate peanut butter cup and wondered where their friend was.

"Do you guys remember why we picked these characters?" Mike asked, never taking his eyes off the road.

"Of course," said Griffin, who definitely hadn't forgotten. The nightmares he'd had all the way up to his first year in college could attest to that. "Made-monsters, because of your story about Doctor Carver."

A chill ran through the car as soon as the name left Griffin's lips.

"Right," said Jonah. "The tearing tear."

"Teratier," Athena corrected. "Mike's silly neologism, but an apt one."

"Huh?"

"It means he made up the word," Athena sighed.

"I found him." Another chill, this one much colder. No one could say for sure if they'd heard Mike right, but somehow, they knew they had.

"What do you mean you found him, exactly?" Griffin asked.

"Well, not literally the guy, but I've been on a few message boards online. Some people theorized Carver must have had a base of operations somewhere here in town, and in between bouts of people calling each other idiots and insulting their respective mothers, there was some actual good detective work going on. I took what they gave me, and I think I tracked down his lab, untouched by the local population all these decades. That's the second part of my surprise. We should go check it out; explore the city like we used to!"

There was hesitation in the air, but no one wanted to speak it out loud.

"Oh, come on!" Mike protested. "I poked around a little and made sure it was safe. No one knows it's there. Carver is a part of our history. When else are we going to have an opportunity like this?"

"Let's do it," said Griffin, earning shocked looks from Athena and Jonah. His boldness surprised him too, but there was something about being with the friends he had during his formative years, the best friends he'd ever had, that made him feel invincible. Besides, Carver had been an itch in the back of his mind for years; it was about time that he scratched it.

Mike drove them to an abandoned water treatment plant nestled between the city's industrial sector and the outskirts of Whisper Falls. He explained that it had been in operation since the late fifties, but was replaced by a state-of-the-art facility five blocks away around four years ago after a terrible rainstorm.

"The fact it's so old means that it has connections to Whisper Falls' old sewer network, the one that got replaced in the eighties. Carver would have played in those tunnels when he was a boy. There's no official record of it, but kids from his time were said to have gone in constantly. The message boards put together that if he had a secret base, one where he wouldn't be found out, it would be there. It would also explain how his creations got around so efficiently; those tunnels run under most of Whisper Falls."

“And we’re just... going in,” Jonah said in disbelief.

“What’s the matter, J? Scared?” Athena teased.

“Are you not?!”

“Of course I am. Any sane person would be. But I’m game if everyone else is.”

“I am,” said Griffin, committing before his compulsion to bail out got the better of him.

Mike showed them inside. Past fields of debris and puddles of water, there was a door which looked like it had been sealed until recently. A guilty-looking crowbar sat on the floor next to it.

“That was me,” Mike admitted. “I didn’t go far, just enough to make sure it was accessible. I brought flashlights. Everyone take one.”

One by one they took a light and followed Mike into the darkness. The tunnels were narrow, just wide enough for them to move single file comfortably, but the ceilings were high and arched. The brickwork was cracked and ancient, coated in mud and moss and grime. Puddles of water lay irregularly along the floor, getting more plentiful as they went.

“Frankenstein didn’t wear the right shoes for this,” Griffin muttered snidely.

“Should we be worried about how sanitary it is down here?” said Athena with growing alarm.

“No,” said Mike. “It’s just been raining on and off tonight. These drains were decommissioned a long time ago. There hasn't been any human waste in this water for years.”

"Now the only human waste in this water is us," Jonah put forward, earning uncomfortable half-laughter from the group.

They kept moving forward, although it didn't take long for it to become apparent that they didn't know what they were doing. Mike had picked up a jagged rock on the way in to leave marks on the walls they could follow back, but there were so many sudden turns and curving pathways, they had begun to see marks they'd left already.

"Maybe it's time we call it a night and start heading back?" Athena suggested.

"What was that?!" Jonah hissed. It was so sudden that everyone froze, before quickly becoming skeptical.

"Very funny, J," huffed Athena.

"I'm serious," he pleaded. "Did you guys not see that? Something was moving up ahead!"

"It was probably just one of our shadows, dude." Griffin meant what he said, but the fear that there was something down here with them began to gnaw at him. And then he, too, saw something out of the corner of his eye, and gnawing turned to biting...

Athena screamed first. Then the rest of them joined her.

Something was in front of them. Its body was partially obscured around a corner, but they all saw it. Skin like an asphyxiated corpse, an uneven mix of blue and purple covered it as if one big bruise. Biceps twice as long as a person's, it leaned on bony forearms which looked like they were breathing. One hand was submerged underwater, but the other dug into the wall, six spindly fingers with razors in place of fingernails. A mop of dark hair covered the top half of its head and face, leaving a gaping hole for a nose exposed, along with a mouth filled with two rows of teeth that was unhinged like a snake's.

"BRAHUK-KUH!" it roared at them. Jonah babbled something no one could understand before lowering his light and running back the way they had come.

"Stay calm!" Mike shouted. "It's—" was all he could say before someone screamed again. The creature had begun to move, a mesmerizing sort of sway as it made its way forward. It was difficult to watch, unnatural in some way their minds couldn't name, so much so that each of them had to take the light off it before they could do anything else.

"Go!" said Griffin, which brought them to their senses. This new danger reignited old programming in him, one he hadn't had need for since his high school days: protect the people you love at all costs.

"What about you?" Athena asked as Griffin began shoving her and Mike in the direction Jonah had gone.

"I'm right behind you! I'm—" Something had come out of the darkness and sliced the back of Griffin's arm from the elbow to his shoulder, making him yelp. He clasped a hand over the wound, dropping his flashlight to do so, and felt warm blood leaking out.

Athena pulled him forward, and intuitively he held onto her since she was now the closest source of light. They ran, losing Mike along the way in the confusion. As they fought to move their feet through progressively deeper water, the sound of screams reverberated off the walls until it was all around them.

"Dammit!" Griffin wailed. "I can't make out any of the markings Mike has been leaving. This place is like a maze without them."

"Quiet," Athena hushed. "If we just keep running around blindly, we're bound to bump into that... thing. If we wait until the yelling gets quieter, we'll know it's probably far away from us. Then we can look for the exit."

"What about Jonah and Mike?"

"You're hurt, and neither of us is equipped to fight monsters. They stand a better chance if we go and get help."

Griffin hesitated, his heart and his head at odds with one another. "Should we dim the light?" he asked after relenting. "Make ourselves harder to spot?"

"It's pitch black without it, and then I think we'd really be dead."

Just as Athena spoke, the flashlight began to dim and flicker.

"You have got to be kidding me..." Griffin said incredulously.

Something else was off, and their blood ran cold when they realized what it was: there hadn't been any screaming for almost a full minute. The two shared one last doomed look before the light went out completely. Impulse compelled them to hold each other, unsure of what to do. They were completely still and silent, which made it easy to make out the sound of splashing coming towards them.

"BRAHUK-KUH!" the darkness screamed, and that sent them running again. Griffin didn't make it far before he collided directly with a wall and knocked himself out.

When he came to, he wasn't sure how much time had passed. His body felt sticky, and he couldn't move. The smell told him they were still in the sewers, disgustingly wet and musty, but with a new underlying scent too, one of chemicals and rotten meat. His pounding head made it hard to form thoughts, but as recent events replayed disjointedly in his mind, his subconscious nagged at him that there was something more to this situation, something that should be obvious if he could just put together the clues.

"Griffin!" Athena's voice. That stirred him. He could only turn his head partially, but he saw Jonah beside him, unconscious and plastered to the wall with some kind of pale, orange gunk. Athena was beyond him, just scarcely visible in Griffin's peripherals, but she appeared to be stuck in the same way.

"W-What's happening?" Griffin mumbled, his head swimming. He looked around and saw they were in a dimly-lit lab of some kind. It was filthy, with mildew and mud everywhere. Several mobile blackboards were scattered around the room, most knocked over and some broken in half. Out of the corner of his eye he could see three large glass tanks, two filled with dark fluid that had shapes barely visible inside. The third was shattered, and suddenly Griffin noticed something that made him scream. The creature that had chased them through the tunnels was glaring at them from behind the other two tanks.

Athena screamed too, but she may not have even realized how much danger they were in; Griffin's gesture could have just given her ignorant, aimless terror somewhere to go. Griffin, meanwhile, couldn't bring himself to look at the hideously deformed thing, but his survival instincts burned whenever he tried to look away, scolding him for taking his eyes off of an obvious predator that meant him harm.

"Shut up!" yelled Mike's voice from somewhere nearby. "You're scaring her!"

'Her?' Griffin thought. 'Not 'it?" That's what made it finally click for him, and he wanted to be sick. Instead, he started to cry.

"Mike!" Athena moaned. "What the hell is going on here?"

"I can explain everything," said Mike, unmistakable guilt in his voice. "Just... god, I thought I was prepared for this... Okay, just let me rant for a second. Why do you think people like Halloween costumes so much?"

"...what?"

"They let us be anyone but ourselves, or at least something other than the facades we put on every day. In a way, dressing up like someone else lets us be our real selves. We should understand that better than anyone by now. We've all grown up, so does getting older mean taking a costume off, or putting one on?"

"What are you talking about, Mike?" Athena asked worriedly.

"We're all older now, and we have to act like adults, but really, aren't we the same people we were in high school? That's where Halloween comes in: costumes feed our delusion that people can change."

"People do change," Griffin fired back. "All the time, every day. Look at Jonah— he's a dad now. As much as I don't want to admit it, I've changed too. I want to stop it, but no one can. So tell me, Mike, what have you turned into? What have you done?!"

"Griffin..." was all Athena could bring herself to say.

"You figured it out, didn't you, buddy?" Mike accused. "Well, you can't tell them! It has to be me who confesses..."

"Tell us what?" said Athena.

"The monster... it's— she's been saying 'breaks' all night. Our codeword for 'something is wrong' or 'I'm not okay.' Athena... that's Olivia."

"...no." Athena sounded like she wanted to vomit. "No, no way." She might have said more, but then she finally saw the beast in the room with them, their friend, and the words choked in her throat.

"How did you figure it out?" Mike shouted, guilt shifting subtly into anger.

"You said you contacted all of us to come back tonight, but you only had four costumes. You must have known Olivia wasn't going to be there, because you knew where she was the whole time. What did you do, Mike?!"

"Nothing! I... Okay, why do we think the story of Doctor Carver is so compelling?"

"Enough with the riddles!"

"This is how I have to explain it!" He was becoming shaky, unhinged. "Carver is a horror story, but people stick to it because, ultimately, the teratier lets us *become* the costume. I kept in touch with Olivia over the years through the internet. She was... unhappy, for a long time. I didn't know how to help her, so I tried just being there for her. When she started talking about finding Carver, I thought she was just roleplaying a little, harkening back to our high school days. But by the time I realized she was in danger, it was too late."

"You found her like this?" Athena surmised.

"She was so... broken. But I had to believe my friend was still in there. That's why I called you guys here, to bring her out of whatever Carver did to her. Once we were in the tunnels, I lured her to us with a trail of candy you didn't notice."

"And the costumes?" asked Griffin.

"I thought maybe... if I reminded her of happier times, like our last Halloween together, it might help."

"Oh god," Athena started to cry. "Olivia... what did they do to you, girl?" The monster responded by trying to hide itself further behind the tanks, devouring some sweets with the wrappers still on.

"What's the plan now, Mike?" Griffin asked critically. He could feel water running down the walls, which was loosening whatever slime was holding him in place. “Prolonged group therapy down here in the sewers? That’s a terrible idea for a lot of reasons, not least of which being that I’m pretty sure the rain is going to flood this place soon.”

“I don’t know, okay?!” Mike started to sob. “I just… I had to do something. How could I leave her like this? We have to help her!”

“Mike…” Athena said pityingly. “This is no life for her. There’s… I can’t believe I’m saying this, but there’s only one way to help her at this point.”

“No!” Mike protested. Griffin noted motion just outside his field of view. “We can rehabilitate her! And then, when *our* Olivia comes back, we can bring her to a doctor, and—”

“Come on, man,” Griffin scoffed. “If the stories about Carver are even a little true, no doctor on Earth could turn her back, not without causing her even more suffering. We need to put her out of her misery.”

“Good luck,” Mike huffed. “I’m pretty sure Carver made her indestructible. And that’s if you could even get her to let you close enough to hurt her.”

Griffin thought for a moment. “I think I know a way.” He fought with all his might to pull himself away from the wall, and that made Olivia hiss and charge at him. Even knowing what he knew now, it was hard not to see his friend as a scary monster. Bright orange saliva dripped from her mouth, and suddenly Griffin understood how they had been glued to the wall.

“Stop!” Mike shouted, appearing from off to the side and throwing himself between Griffin and Olivia. “It’s okay! It’s me, Liv. You know me, and you know Griffin. He’s just trying to help.”

With a prolonged and sticky ‘THUCK’ sound, Griffin pried himself free and got to his feet. It was still difficult to move, but he reached a hand into the pocket of his Frankenstein shirt and fished out a handful of the candy they had collected earlier in the evening. Keeping Olivia firmly in his peripherals, he scattered it in front of her. He could see her sizing him up, like a vicious dog being fed by an unfamiliar human. But then she gathered up the pieces before running off somewhere into the darkness.

“Her peanut allergy,” said Griffin wistfully, still looking in the direction she had gone. “There’s enough in there that should do the trick.”

“Why did I just let you do that?” Mike asked, more to himself than anyone else.

“Because deep down you know we couldn’t do anything better for her,” said Athena. “And speaking of the best we can do for people, can somebody please get me off this godforsaken wall before we’re all underwater?”

The floor was flooding in various places. Griffin and Mike awkwardly pried Athena free, and while she and Mike did the same for the unconscious Jonah, Griffin took his first proper look at their surroundings. It was a lab, alright, incredibly old and disheveled, but with signs of upkeep too. Someone had been coming back here recently; Griffin couldn’t be certain that it was Carver, but that was the simplest explanation. When he thought about what

Carver had done to Olivia, potentially others as well, a sickening anger overtook Griffin and twisted his stomach into a knot. Desperately he scanned the ground for something big and blunt, settling on a rusty pipe that was bent at one end.

He started swinging the second it was in his hand, only containing himself enough to avoid hitting the remaining tanks like the kind Olivia had seemingly emerged from. If there was even a chance that something like what she had become could be alive in there, not all the rage in the world could have made him break one. He saved his fury for the rest of the lab, with machines either clanging lifelessly or sparking and garbling in protest of his assault. Walls of beakers and glass tubes and rubber hoses shattered and toppled before him, their contents splashing back onto his face and chest. It stung, but only minimally, which made Griffin realize that Olivia's saliva had numbed his body somewhat.

"Griff!" Mike shouted, catching him by the arm. Griffin wanted to argue, but he began to gather why Mike had chosen now to object. Something Griffin had knocked over had collapsed a brick wall, and now the water was flooding in at an alarming speed.

"We need to get out of here," Athena said while propping up Jonah.

"I'm staying," Mike said desolately.

"What?!"

"I… I can't let Olivia die alone. I may not have been able to prevent her fate, but it's something. Maybe then I can be forgiven for my mistakes."

"We don't have time for this," Athena groaned. "You want forgiveness? Fine, you have it. I forgive you, Griffin forgives you, and Olivia—"

"Let him stay," Griffin said coldly. "He's right. She shouldn't be alone." He shared a long, hard look with Mike, but neither of them said anything more to one another.

"What?" Athena gasped. "No, we're not just gonna leave—"

"You better hurry," Mike interrupted. "It would be hard to find your way out of here even without Jonah weighing you down, and the rain must really be coming down now if this place is sinking so fast."

Griffin began to support Jonah too, ignoring any further objections Athena made as they left. She continued to plead with Mike until he was completely out of view, but Griffin never looked back.

"So, you just left him there?" Jonah asked after recovering in their motel room. The desk clerk had looked at them suspiciously all through check-in, skeptical that they had just come from a Halloween party, which was their excuse for why they looked and smelled so bad, but he ultimately handed over the key without fuss or accusation.

"I did," Griffin said, stifling a cocktail of guilt and regret that was bubbling up inside him. "I didn't think I had it in me, but I guess I was right... people do change. Maybe I'm still changing, because I don't feel bad."

“It wasn’t his fault,” Athena sighed, who had been staring out the window for the entirety of Griffin’s recap, only chiming in occasionally to add details Griffin had missed.

“He wasn’t blameless!” Griffin growled, more aggressive than he had intended. He offered Athena an apologetic shrug that went unheeded. “He didn’t deserve to die, but I guess I didn’t feel compelled to save him, either. Not if that’s how he wanted to go.”

“Savage,” Jonah mused, somewhere between condemnation and admiration. “You got a few scars to match your new persona there, Griff. Or you will, if that mug of yours ever heals. Gonna need a scary mask like the bad guy in a cheap horror flick.”

Griffin studied his face in a mirror. “It really hurts. I think this orange crud is starting to wear off.”

“Heh, monster spit,” Jonah chuckled.

“Don’t call her that!” Athena shouted. “Her name was Olivia Selick, and she was our friend. No matter what Carver did to her, he could never change that. He wasn’t that good! He’s the real monster here, not Olivia.”

They sat in silence for a long time. “You know,” said Jonah, breaking the quiet, “that’s the really scary part here.”

“What is?” asked Griffin.

“Well, none of us saw Carver, but he must still be out there. *Someone* did that stuff to Olivia. So, we’re at the end of the horror movie, just before the credits roll, where they reveal the monster is still alive, ready to wreak havoc again in the sequel. Those ones always scared me the most.”

More silence, this time even more uncomfortable.

"I think you're basically right," Griffin said eventually. "But not in the way you think." He paused, but they simply waited patiently for him to continue. "There is a monster lurking before the credits, but we have more control over the script than you realize."

Griffin admired the marks on his face more closely, smiling for the first time since before they had gone into the sewers. "Maybe I *should* get a mask, Jonah— a really scary one. After all, there's lots of things that go bump in the night."

"What's your point, Griffin?" Athena asked anxiously.

"I think it's time someone gave them a reason to be afraid of the dark."

Grim Grinning Gods Gathered in a Graveyard

Gamesmanship (noun) – distinct from sportsmanship, the art or practice of winning games by any means necessary, however questionable, without actually violating any rules.

It was a chaotic time in the Willows household. A chain of events had begun when Bear Willows, the family dog, killed a raccoon which had wandered into their backyard. Said act of senseless violence and animal instinct would go on to disrupt the plans of everyone else in the homestead.

Mr. Willows, who originally intended to hand out candy to trick-or-treaters while dressed as Frankenstein's monster, now had to find a secluded spot in the woods to dispose of Bear's victim, seeing as any creature buried in their own backyard would just be dug up again. Later on, Mr. Willows would laugh at the bizarro nature of his task, the monster burying a corpse instead of the doctor exhuming one. With his sudden unavailability, that left candy duty to Mrs. Willows, who had wanted, nay, needed to take their son David out that night.

"You'll just have to do it, Bethany," she said sternly to her daughter. "It isn't fair to your brother if he misses out."

"Oh, but it's fair to me that I miss out on spending time with Sam?"

"Careful with that tone." Mrs. Willows issued her warning through narrowed eyes. "And no one said you couldn't see Sam. Bring them along. David adores Sam."

"But... we're both so exhausted!" Beth whined.

"And whose fault is that?"

"Hey, you said no parties on Halloween, and I listened to you. A party the night before is a good compromise, I think."

"You're taking him," sighed Beth's mother, pinching the bridge of her nose in frustration. "That's final."

"But—"

"No buts, Bethany!" Mrs. Willows' tone had changed completely, jumping from annoyed to ferocious with just three words. She grabbed her daughter's arm, harder than either of them thought she should have, and dragged her in front of the fridge, out of earshot of the stairs, and thus out of earshot of David's room.

"Now you listen and you listen good," she continued, screaming through a whisper. "I am done playing around, okay? That little boy loves Halloween, and with God as my witness, we are going to give him the best Halloween night he's ever had, do you understand me? I don't care that you're hungover, I don't care that you have other things you'd rather be doing. You are going to take your brother trick-or-treating and make sure he has a good time, you selfish, spoiled, brat."

Bethany's chest went up and down as she tried to steady her shaky breathing, a sure sign that tears weren't far behind. While she kept herself from sobbing, her eyes did get wet. Mrs. Willows regarded her with a wall of hostility, one which quickly melted like a Kit Kat bar in the tight grip of an oblivious child.

"Sweetie, I'm sorry," she relented, wrapping her arms around Beth and beginning to cry herself. There was a significant pause before Beth reciprocated the hug, as she slowly came to the conclusion that being angry at her mother and being sympathetic for all the devastating pressure she'd been under recently were not mutually exclusive feelings.

"I think I'm ready," said David, hurrying down the stairs in his black onesie adorned with the model of a skeleton. He had expressed disappointment after discovering that the plastic bones, which glowed in the dark, were only on one side. It was not even significant disappointment, tantamount more so to getting the wrong color pencil case for school than to not getting the Christmas present he was hoping for, but Mrs. Willows still went out of her way to go back to Shopper Mart and buy a second one, which she promptly stitched together so you could tell he was a skeleton no matter which way you looked at the costume.

"You look amazing, honey," said Mrs. Willows after discreetly rubbing her eyes.

"Is Dad back from burying the raccoon yet?

"W-What? Who told you...?" She looked accusingly at Beth, who shrugged before leaving the kitchen to get her coat. "Oh, honey. I guess you heard us talking, huh? Yeah, Bear had a little... accident in the backyard."

"It's okay, Mom." If the prospect of a family member, even a canine one, murdering a small creature put any kind of damper on David Willows' spirits, he showed no sign of it. "I know Bear didn't mean to." He went over to the corner where the German shepherd had been sulking and gave him a pat on the head. Bear returned the gesture by licking David's face enthusiastically, happy to be receiving affection after being iced out all night by the other members of the family.

"Your sister will be taking you out tonight... is that okay?"

"But Beth wants to go to Sam's to watch horror movies and cuddle," David said matter-of-factly. His sister blushed as if this had been some kind of secret, although she didn't deny it.

"I thought you hated horror movies?" observed Mrs. Willows.

"Sam likes them..." Beth smiled. "Some of them are actually decent."

"Well, regardless, she's happy to take you, David." She looked at her daughter as she spoke, mouth smiling but eyes intense and expectant. "Aren't you, Bethany?"

"Uh-huh. Whaddya say, squirt? Wanna go meet Sam?"

"Yeah!"

"You guys get two hours tops, okay? That means in exactly two hours from now you are walking back through that door, got it?"

"We got it," the siblings said in unison, having been on the receiving end of their mother's 'got it?'s many times.

"Be safe, honey," she said to David. "Button up your jacket if it gets too cold, and tell your sister if you get one of your headaches so she can bring you home."

Mrs. Willows bid her children farewell, watching them go until they disappeared around the bend at the end of their street. She was crying again by the time the first trick-or-treaters arrived.

David was completely fascinated by Sam's Freddy Krueger costume. They'd worn it the night before to the party with Beth, who had done their makeup to look more like Krueger's trademark burned visage. Now it was heavily wrinkled and stained with sweat, and Sam's face was completely barren underneath a ratty fedora. There was a kind of taboo appeal David found with 'big kid movies,' although he had only ever seen five minutes of *Friday the 13th*, and that had given him nightmares for three days.

"We'll induct you into the club someday, little man," Sam laughed. "There's this one gruesome bit in *The Exorcist* you'll love. You see, Linda Blair..."

"Easy there, Romero," Beth warned cheerfully.

"Hey, I'm not showing him the movie, am I?"

"No, but you're a very vivid storyteller." The pair laughed and pulled each other in close for a kiss. David pretended to gag and turned away, but deep down he liked how happy Sam made his sister.

The trio covered a lot of ground in just half an hour. They were using an old map of the neighborhood that Beth had made when she was David's age. The yellowed paper held together with childhood dreams and scotch tape laid out a path that went out from the Willows house in a spiral pattern, labeling crosswalks, streets with no sidewalk, and houses that gave out fruit or dental floss in lieu of candy (the latter being marked with thick black X's). The map was a point of nostalgic pride for Beth, one she was happy to share with her brother. So, when he asked if they could deviate from her time-tested trail, she got a little impatient.

"There's no way I'm trekking up Ashley Street," she told him. "I'm exhausted, and that incline is brutal."

"Cmon, Beth!" David protested. "Jeremy told me there are secret rich people on this street. They have the good stuff!"

"I said no."

"I can take him," Sam put forward innocently. "You rest up here. I'm sure David is willing to part with some of his candy as recompense." They winked at the tiny skeleton, who was grinning happily.

"Sure!" said the skeleton. "A pack of Twizzlers?"

"Three packs, since they're the tiny ones," Beth haggled. "And be grateful it isn't more. You're a skeleton. That means you don't even have a stomach to put them in."

David and Sam quickly learned why Beth had been so reluctant to come up this way. The steep slope made their calves start to hurt after just three houses, but neither of them acknowledged it out loud. Suspicions had been proven true when numerous full-sized candy bars were deposited into the plastic jack-o'-lantern David carried. There was something off about this particular street, though. David noticed it first, then Sam soon after.

Ashley Street was a cul-de-sac, meaning there was no exit at the end. Therefore, the kids on the other side of the road were moving in the opposite direction. Despite that making for a more favorable incline, which should have sped the steps of the costumed children who walked there, everyone trudged at a slow, listless pace. Heads were hung, bags of candy were frighteningly empty, if not completely absent. A few of them were crying.

The point where the changeover seemed to happen was a gathering of children and teenagers where the incline of the street nearly reached its peak. Standing in the center was a man of indeterminate age, looking like he could be anywhere from mid-thirties to early sixties. His skin was pale and sallow, and his smile looked a little too large for his face. Yellow eyes gazed out from overtop a pair of old-fashioned pince-nez glasses. He wore a jet-black scarf, a midnight blue bowler hat with a cherry red band, and shoes with a checkerboard pattern on them. His most striking article of clothing, though, was a golden suit jacket which shone wickedly in the streetlights. It was adorned with the four suits of playing cards, and looked as if it were made of metal, but still moved like fabric.

"Fancy a wager, anyone?" he posed to the gathered crowd. "Why waste your time trick-or-treating when you could triple, no, quadruple your candy acquisition with just one simple bet?" He gestured behind him to a sack that could put the great Saint Nick to shame, made of burlap and filled so full that you could see a high fructose heaven through the fabric. Smarties and suckers, Hershey chocolate and Haribo gummies; there looked to be no end to the variety the bag contained.

"I want to try!" David announced happily to Sam. "If we win some candy, we can get off of this street and be home in time for Charlie Brown!"

"Beware of Greeks bearing gifts, little man."

"What?"

"I'm saying you always gotta be skeptical about free candy," Sam laughed.

"There's no such thing as free when you gamble with the Gamesman, mister," said the strangely dressed man. "Wagers are made, and prizes are won— that is the nature of the transaction."

"I'm great at games," bragged the young skeleton. "This will be a piece of cake. Let's do it!"

"Splendid," chirped the Gamesman. "Let's start with something small, shall we? Let's say... half my candy versus half your candy?"

"That sounds good," said David, his optimism not shared by Sam.

"Then the wager is made!" The Gamesman reached into his coat pocket and produced a small pile of trading cards, which were the color of dark emeralds and lined with silver. "The game is simple, boy-o. Find the lucky rabbit." He flipped one of the cards around to reveal the red silhouette of a rabbit. After flipping it back, the cards were shuffled for a few seconds with a disturbing level of finesse before being fanned out and presented to David.

"That one!" David declared with assured triumph. The card he turned around, though, bore the image of a skull, which laughed at him by some sort of hologram effect.

"Oh, tough luck," moaned the Gamesman insincerely. David's jack-o'-lantern wobbled as half its contents disappeared, and the hefty bag of candy shifted with added volume. "Put that frown away, though. The Gamesman is nothing if not courteous. I'll give you a chance at redemption, young man. A new game, double or nothing. What do you say?"

"David…" Sam cautioned.

"O-kay," David agreed. Something about losing half his night's work in an instant made his face hot, filled with a secret shame that an eleven-year-old couldn't fully comprehend.

"Wonderful." The last syllable he spoke was stretched to an uncomfortable degree. "This next game is pretty simple. Guess what number I'm thinking."

"Hey!" barked Sam. "That's not fair. How's he s'posed to—?"

"It's okay." David held up a hand to silence his friend. Eyes narrowed at his opponent, the boy drew a breath and waited for his target to come to him. "Twenty-three… point forty-two," he said at last.

“That’s impossible...” muttered the Gamesman, whose eyes had gone wide enough to give Sam and David similar concerns about them bulging out of his head. What shocked them just as much was when the sack of candy began to float in the air, drifting several feet until it landed at David’s side.

“How did you do that?!” the Gamesman suddenly snapped. Half the assembly backed away with this change in tone. “There was no way you could have guessed that number. What are you?”

“My name’s David, and if you’re going to be a sore loser, we’re just going to leave.”

“Yeah,” Sam added smugly. “My boy David here is about to be very popular.”

“I very much doubt that.” The Gamesman’s voice was quiet now, almost growling at a whisper. Giving no sign of what he was about to do, he abruptly punched David square in the face, knocking him back nearly a foot and onto his backside. “Sorry, kid. You did win... somehow, but at the end of the day there’s still good old-fashioned theft.”

Things happened in a blur after that for everyone involved. Sam had immediately run to David to see if he was okay, giving the Gamesman plenty of time to grab the bag of candy, haul it over his shoulder, and run off into the night. Completely shocked by what had just transpired, Sam could think of nothing else to do but pick David up in their arms and go find Beth. The plastic jack-o’-lantern was left behind in the street, empty and cracked down the middle of its face.

They found Beth where they had left her, sitting on a large white rock on the edge of someone's lawn. As soon as she saw the pair, she shot to her feet. After a brief inquiry to confirm David wasn't grievously injured, Sam recited as succinct a summary of events as they could.

"'The Gamesman?'" David's sister repeated back. "Really?"

"I dunno," Sam lamented. "He was some kind of freak, okay?"

"Beth?" David whimpered, still in Sam's arms. His words were shaky, like he was fighting the urge to cry.

"Yeah, buddy, I'm here. It's okay."

"Can we just go home?"

"What?"

"I know it was dumb to make a bet with that guy," he blubbered. "I'm sorry. I've already kept you out long enough. We should just go home and cut our losses."

"David..."

"All that candy probably would have wrecked my teeth anyway."

There was something about the way David looked in this moment that affected Beth deeply. There was a snot bubble lodged inelegantly in one of his nostrils. His teeth were chattering, likely as much due to being upset as it was the chilly October evening. A few choice tears had begun rolling down his cheeks. Worst of all, though, was the black eye forming on the right side of his face, sure to be a shiner which could put some boxers to shame. Sincerely speaking, he looked pathetic, and that made Beth inexorably angry.

Something changed in the oldest Willows child. The remnants of her hangover had been like a fog, now suddenly and violently burned away by the fury building in the pit of her stomach. Their parents wanted nothing more than to give David a good Halloween; it was the only thing that mattered to them, and for good reason. While the onus would never entirely fall upon a sibling the way it did a parent, she was still his big sister, and she had failed to protect her brother when he'd needed her most. Shame carried her other emotions forward, pushing them to their natural, outraged extremes.

"Screw that!" she exclaimed with more volume than she had probably intended, garnering unfavorable looks from the various costume-wearing passersby. David and Sam snapped to attention, neither of them having heard Beth curse so aggressively before, even if it was a mild one. "Some jerk who dresses like he works in the world's worst casino thinks he can steal our Halloween? He's got another thing coming!"

"Beth," said Sam, equal parts afraid and enamored. "I agree that it's a raw deal, but like... it's just candy, y'know?" David nodded in agreement rapidly, his body reacting to his sister's outburst like he was the one in trouble, even though she was on his side.

“It isn’t just candy!” she shot back. “It’s the principle of the thing. How many other kids are going home empty-handed tonight because of this creep? Who’s to say he hasn’t given out more black eyes? Or done worse? You two can go home if you want, but I’m not coming back until I’ve got a bag full of Milky Ways, Jolly Ranchers, and the Gamesman’s manhood.”

Without waiting for a response, Beth spun around and stormed off. She made it as far as the next crosswalk before freezing, fighting with herself to accept the realization that she was afraid. The full scope of the circumstances she was in weren’t fully known to her, but she feared what would unravel if she pulled on this thread.

When she turned around, Sam was putting David down, and David was wiping his nose and his good eye with the sleeve of his costume. When they noticed her staring at them, their gaze fell to the ground.

“Well, are you coming?” she asked expectantly, and the pair hurried to catch up with her. As they walked, David tugged on his sister’s coat.

“Beth?” he asked, his voice now a little more even. “Are you going to kill the Gamesman?”

“We’ll see,” she said plainly, not looking at her brother or stopping for even a second.

The trio had better luck than they thought they might when it came to tracking their adversary. Sam was sure they had seen the Gamesman run up the road, not back down. Ashley Street may have ended in a circle, but the backmost houses bordered a small ravine which, according to Beth's map, opened up right next to Knudsen Avenue. If they circled around that way, they might nearly cut him off. Once they were in that vicinity, it was simply a matter of asking around for leads.

A robot and a pirate were absolutely distraught over the recent loss of their candy, and it was easy to deduce after a quick consultation that they'd had a run-in with the Gamesman. The group was pointed in the direction of Walker Cemetery, the oldest graveyard in Whisper Falls. They approached the gates, but David pulled back before they could enter.

"Do we have to go in there, Beth?"

"Yeah!" she ardently declared. "That's where the bad guy is hiding. If we're sneaky, we can get the jump on him. What are you afraid of, buddy?"

"...zombies," he admitted after a short pause. Sam couldn't help but snort, and Beth shot them a scolding look. "Halloween is when monsters and other spooky things get to walk around like the rest of us. The kids in class said so."

"David, that's just—" began his sister.

"That's just it," Sam interrupted. "Monsters do roam free on Halloween, but that's why we wear costumes. To trick them."

"Really?" An awed realization filled the young boy's voice.

"Yeah, and you've got the best trick of all. You're a skeleton. Zombies don't like skeletons, because there's no meat on their bones. No zombie is gonna touch you in there!"

"But what about Beth?" David asked. Sam looked at their girlfriend and studied her for a moment.

"She's okay too. Beth is scarier than the zombies." David laughed, and Beth punched Sam in the arm. Despite the gesture, she was smiling, grateful that Sam could calm David down and help him find his courage.

A thick mist hung on the ground. City lights from outside the perimeter provided minimal illumination, but the cemetery itself was completely unlit, creating a dark square in the middle of the city. If it weren't for the Gamesman's garish jacket, they may not have spotted him slinking between the tombstones.

"What do we do now?" whispered David. The group had an excellent vantage point, peering out from behind a decrepit columbarium.

"We should wait," Beth advised. "We don't know what he's doing here. If he's just hiding, we can jump him, but he might have friends."

"You can come out now," the Gamesman called, which made the trio's blood run cold. David looked to Beth for guidance, who in turn looked to Sam, only to see that they were eying her anxiously.

“Wait,” was all she could think to say. Their target wasn’t actually looking in their direction at all; did he really notice them?

“Oh, don’t be difficult,” the Gamesman continued, seemingly addressing the air itself. “Fine,” he huffed, holding out his arms like a cheerleader asking the crowd to give him a ‘Y.’

“I beseech you!” he shouted, his demeanor now stark and gracious. “With respect and admiration, please appear before me now. I beg you, grant me an audience!”

At first, the only response he got was a choir of crickets, but then the ground started to shake. David instinctively clutched Beth’s right hand, and with her left she did the same thing to Sam. A dogged wind had picked up, evident by the rolling fog. Four pale, orange spotlights suddenly materialized around the Gamesman, inexplicably subtle and blinding at the same time. The trio could make out shapes in them, nearly human silhouettes which stood imposingly as they took form. A massive grave marker just outside the circle carved to resemble an armchair received its own spotlight, one which drew the mist into it.

“I don’t believe it,” Sam gasped after the spotlights faded.

“What?” asked Beth, fearing she was missing some fatal detail based on the transfixed look on her partner’s face.

“Finally,” the Gamesman said indignantly to the four figures who stood around him. There was a little boy in a fall jacket holding a blue balloon. One was a woman dressed like a classic storybook witch, complete with pointy black hat and striped stockings. Her face looked neither old nor young, every angle conveying a different age. There was a person in a dark hood and cloak, their only defining feature being a featureless white mask. For as dark as the graveyard was, the space around this one seemed just a little darker. The fourth figure was the most bizarre, wearing a costume made up of dozens of other costume pieces, looking as if they were chosen and put on with no rhyme or reason. Their shape was the least distinct, at times looking more like a pile than a person.

"We come when we're called, Gamesman," said the little boy.

"One need only ask nicely," the hooded figure hissed.

"Have you brought what we asked for?" the witch asked excitedly.

"Yes, I—"

"This will not clear the debt," barked the mass of masks, gloves, and hats. "But pray that it lessens your burden."

"Can I get a word in?" the Gamesman snapped back. "Yes, I have done what you asked. Six hundred and sixty-six pieces of candy, as ordered. Plus a little extra, as a sign of good faith."

"Faith is not our concern, fool," said the hooded figure.

“Such a lovely bag,” the witch salivated over the sack placed before them. “Your tricks are our treats.”

“Actually, they're ours!” Beth shouted, revealing the trio's position.

“No, wait!” Sam urged. They reached out for the hand which had just unclasped theirs, but Beth was already on the move.

“I don't know what sort of deal you have with this creep, but he assaulted my little brother and ran off with his hard-earned candy. We want it back.”

“Children,” the little boy observed.

“Angry children,” added the masked man.

“Beth...” whispered Sam, approaching her from behind while David followed closely.

“Who’s in charge?” the Willows girl demanded. “Who am I having words with?”

All four of the mysterious figures turned their heads towards the grave with the throne, which at some point had ceased to be empty. In it sat a scarecrow that was nearly nine feet tall. It wore a tattered plaid shirt, black overalls, and a chocolate brown hat, whose style could be described as a cross between the classic witch hat and a fedora. It didn’t move, save for the flame in its jack-o’-lantern head.

“One doesn’t really have words with Spirit, dearie,” said the witch.

"He listens, and makes his intentions known accordingly," brayed the walking costume store bargain bin.

"Nice eye, kid," the Gamesman taunted, flashing a toothy grin towards David. Beth shot forward, not entirely sure what would happen if she closed the gap between herself and her brother's attacker. She wouldn't have to learn just yet, though, because Sam held her back.

"Babe, stop." The entire Willows family had, at some point, used terms like 'chill' or 'easy-going' when describing Sam. There was an uncharacteristic coldness to them now, though there was no malice in it. David thought it reminded him of the way his father had acted on a camping trip two years ago when the young boy got too close to a family of bears. He had been almost aggressive when he told David to get back, but it was only because he knew his son was in danger.

"This one knows us," said the one in the hood.

"What are your names?" asked the little boy.

"I'm Beth. This is Sam, and my brother, David. Who the hell are you?"

"The one you call Sam knows us," cackled the witch. "Why don't you ask them?"

Beth's body finally softened a little, and she turned to face Sam. She looked at them with eyes caught between accusation and confusion.

"Not personally," Sam admitted, rubbing the back of their neck and not making eye contact with anyone. “I recognize them from a book I read as a kid, though. These... are the gods of Halloween.”

“You’ve got to be joking.”

“I’m not. I don’t know how, but... it’s them; I just feel it. That’s Sarah Swete,” they gestured to the witch. “Original architect of the house made of candy. She’s the inventor of the candy apple... and the poisoned candy apple.”

“You flatter me, dearie,” the witch beamed. Her face blushed a shade of green, and she did a half-curtsy.

“That... thing,” Sam continued, “is Garb. They have no physical form of their own. If you’ve ever lost a piece of your costume while out trick-or-treating, chances are it’s been a part of Garb’s body at one point or another. The guy in the hood is the Violent Dark. He’s... I always forget his specifics.”

“Fear, child,” said the masked man, who seemed to materialize inches from Sam’s face, separating them from Beth and making David scream. “I am the unknown danger that lurks just outside the glow of the streetlight. I am the shine of a blade in the stygian night. The slashers in your horror films all worship at my church. The hairs on the back of your neck stand at attention when my presence is felt, but not yet known. I am the Violent Dark, and I am what it means to be afraid.”

“Right...” said Sam. They never took their eyes off the horror god, circling around them back to Beth and taking David with them. After the trio took several steps to the side, Sam finally looked at the little boy.

"That must mean you're...?"

"I'm afraid so."

"You're shorter than I expected."

"Who is he?" David pleaded.

"That's Death, buddy."

"Death?" David stared at the little boy, eyes wide and head tilted just slightly.

"Yup. Halloween is when the veil between our human world and the world beyond is at its thinnest. Death is a big part of Halloween."

"I'm a big part of all things," said the boy with the balloon. "But I don't like to make a fuss."

"The guy in the chair is Spirit O'Halloween," Sam said with rekindled admiration. "You've heard of people having 'holiday spirit'? Well, that guy is the spirit. Anytime you got a fuzzy feeling in your stomach because you loved Halloween just so darn much, Spirit was there."

"Great," Beth sighed insincerely. "That's... wow, that's a lot to process. But alright, what's that got to do— David!"

The improbability of what Sam was describing had momentarily distracted Beth from the fact that her brother had wandered towards the little boy that Sam had identified as the Grim Reaper.

"Why do you look like a kid?" David asked.

"That's a strange question," the little boy replied. "Do you ask your sister why she looks like your sister? Or your mom and dad why they look the way they do?"

"I suppose not, sorry. I like your balloon."

"Thank you!" Death replied cheerily. "I'm fond of your skeleton costume. Not anatomically correct, of course, but I can see how that might be fun."

"Mom said an ana... anatomically correct costume wouldn't be practical."

"David, get away from him!" Beth stomped over and forcefully grabbed David's hand with the intention of pulling him away. Her eyes met with Death's, and for a moment she took him to be just an ordinary, unassuming little boy. A small twinge of shame came over her for potentially scaring a child she didn't know by scolding her little brother in front of him. "Sorry, I—"

"There's no need to apologize, Bethany Willows," Death interrupted in an excessively polite way which made Beth's skin crawl. Knowing her full name didn't do anything to put her at ease. "Everyone makes friends with me eventually. Young David here was just getting a head start. Good thing, too, on account of the—"

"Shut up!" Beth shrieked. As she dragged David back towards Sam, she had to dart around Sarah Swete and the Violent Dark, who were watching them with eager stances. "How does my brother's Halloween candy factor into... whatever is happening here? What *is* even happening here?"

"The Gamesman chose to challenge us two seasons past," said Garb. "The wretched dog overestimated his abilities, and in failing to best us, he is now in our debt."

"We all have ways of having him pay off his arrears," giggled Sarah Swete. "Mine usually involves candy!"

"Yes, and I provided a veritable mountain of that sugary garbage to you. Nearly seven hundred pieces of it, all won fair and square."

"Actually, David won it," Sam pointed out. "You just beat him up when he won your impossible game."

"Stealing candy from children, assaulting a smaller and weaker opponent," the Violent Dark laughed. "And now we find out you're a sore loser? You really are pathetic, aren't you?"

"That may be," said Death, "but this is a grave offense being described. "Do you deny it, Gamesman?"

"Of course I don't," he said shamelessly. "But it was all a game. I played with everything I had at my disposal. It isn't my fault that the brat couldn't hold onto his winnings."

"You're scared of me," said David. Everyone, mortal or otherwise, looked at David with varying combinations of surprise and amusement. "You're scared of what I can do, how I beat you earlier. That's why you hit me, and that's why you're talking down to me now; it's to make yourself seem strong, but you just look weak."

“You loathsome wretch!” the Gamesman screamed. He looked as if he might descend on the Willows boy, but a long piece of curved and jagged metal emerged from the cloak of the Violent Dark, barring him from moving forward like an arm on the world’s deadliest toll booth.

“It is you who is the wretch, Gamesman,” said Garb. “Because of your actions, your offering is now in dispute!”

“Can’t refute it’s in dispute!” babbled Sarah.

“There’s only one who can decide what must be done,” Death reminded the others. They turned to face their master, the motionless scarecrow presiding over the proceedings. A fierce but brief wind blew, and suddenly two scrolls made from pale orange paper and tied with black ribbon were in each of Spirit's hands. “There we are.”

“What does that mean?” Beth asked. “He didn’t do anything.”

“Oh, but he did,” hissed the Violent Dark. Sarah Swete clapped her hands in excitement, but said nothing.

“Gamesman,” Death addressed. “Seeing as you cannot yet count the acquired candy against your debt, we command you to use your powers for one last game, one whose terms are set by us.”

“Very well.”

“Do you still desire what was taken, children?” Beth looked to David and Sam before they all nodded. “Then the game is as follows. The

Gamesman will take one scroll; you will take the other. Each is a list of five things, all pertaining to one of us. The objective is to find as many items from the list as possible in one hour and bring them back here. No side shall take action to impede the other. Whoever most superbly carries out their task will be the winner. Do the assembled parties each agree to these terms?"

"I do," griped the Gamesman.

"We just get the candy?" Beth probed. "Seems like a small prize now, given all the baloney we've had to put up with tonight."

"Plus, it's ours anyway!" clamored David, inspired by his sister's boldness.

"Yeah!" punctuated Sam.

"Not to mention the fact that it's getting late. If we play this game, we could be putting ourselves in danger. And then there's the worry it will give our poor mother." Beth felt a sense of pride in her skills at bargaining, or perhaps it was just relief that the time she spent in debate club hadn't been a waste.

"Smart girl," huffed the Violent Dark.

"If you win," said Death, "you may also ask one favor of this collective. If it is within our power, you shall have it."

"Hold on," the Gamesman interrupted. "If they're getting a bonus, so should I."

"Your impudence is staggering," bellowed Garb.

"He makes an apt point, though," Death acknowledged. "Very well, Gamesman. Should you succeed, with the candy that's been provided, we will consider your debt paid."

"That's more like it! I agree."

"Us too."

Beth and the Gamesman each approached Spirit O'Halloween, the former only just now appreciating the stature of the holiday icon. The two took their scrolls in tandem, and the second they did so, the fog began to roll back in. The gods of Halloween became one with it, each in their own time.

"Good luck," whispered the wind in all of their voices.

"This will be too easy," the Gamesman laughed. "I almost feel sorry for you children. Almost."

"Well, I do feel sorry for you," said David. "Anyone as mean as you must be pretty sad inside."

"My man David is speaking the truth," Sam admired. "What even are you? Stealing candy from kids on Halloween is a special kind of messed up. You're not just some ordinary psycho, are you?"

"I think you'll find I'm an extraordinary psycho," sneered the man in the gold jacket.

"How'd you take my candy?" David asked with youthful candor. "The first time, I mean. It just disappeared from my bucket like magic."

"It was magic, you imbecile."

"Careful how you talk to my little brother," Beth admonished.

"None of you know who you're up against," said the Gamesman. "I may have been reduced to a holiday scoundrel this year, but my exploits stretch far beyond your imaginations. I'm older than your parents, or even your grandparents. Hundreds have gamed with me, betting not just their material possessions and wealth, but their skills, their natural talents, even years off their lives. All to win more of the same from me. I contain multitudes. All of you are beneath me."

"We'll see about that." Beth took David by the hand and led him out of the graveyard with Sam following. She felt no need to say anything more to their opponent; their performance in the game would speak volumes.

The writing on the inside of the scroll looked like it had been cut rather than written. The letters glowed like embers expelled from a campfire. Most of it was crowded at the top, leaving a majority of the paper blank.

"'Items pop up one by one,'" David read. "'So that way you have more fun.'"

"'Should you ask for item new,'" Sam continued. "'Your opponent sees it too.' What does that mean?"

“I’m guessing that we have the option to skip ahead in the list,” said Beth. “But if we do, that means the Gamesman also gets to.”

“So, we need to be careful,” assessed her little brother.

“Right. ‘For your first, exciting task, a piece of candy’s what we ask.’ This must be Sarah Swete’s item.”

“‘But not just any boring treat,’” read Sam. “‘A unique snack that can’t be beat. Confectionery that’s seldom seen, on this, the night of Hallowe’en.’”

It took Beth all of thirteen seconds to think of an answer. Her map once again proved to be immeasurably useful tonight. There was a single house that had the unique marker of a Christmas tree on it. She explained that this was the house of Mrs. McCready. Every year, stores and other businesses would introduce their Christmas merchandise earlier and earlier, encroaching on the Halloween decor like holiday tectonic plates. Mrs. McCready, both inventive and thrifty, took this as an opportunity to do something different.

The treats were called ‘peppermint twists,’ and consisted of ground up candy canes, gingerbread cookie dough, cinnamon powder, and just a dollop of sugar frosting. Beth had eaten one once when she was younger, and they hadn’t been bad, but they just didn’t fit the Halloween mood, and that had made them seem worse in retrospect. What was even stranger was the fact that Mrs. McCready refused to actually make them in December. Despite the woman’s strange idiosyncrasies, she was thrilled to receive the trio when they showed up and said they had to have a peppermint twist right away. Unsurprisingly, there were plenty left.

"One down, four to go," David happily observed. "Whoa, the letters are just kind of appearing."

"That must mean the Gamesman is falling behind," said Beth.

"Or he's waiting for us to progress so he can see more items," Sam speculated.

"'It's not how much that you can fund,'" read David. "'Find me what has been abandoned. Search through shelves in wholesale haunts, for costume pieces no one wants.'"

"Garb," said Sam. "We're collecting pieces for Garb's body. I think I know where to go."

Along the way, Sam explained that they worked at the local Shopper Mart last year, and on the night of October 31st, they moved all the unsold Halloween stuff into one big bin before assembling the Christmas trees for display. The store was mostly deserted when they got there, save for Phil, who was thankfully an employee that Sam was still on friendly terms with.

"Hey man, you mind if we dig through the costumes?" Sam asked. "We're kind of on a mission."

"Dude, I'm working late on Halloween, running on three hours of sleep, and grappling with a faux fir. You could set the store on fire and I probably wouldn't notice or care."

Sam explained that when they were little and read about the gods of Halloween, Garb had been their favorite, since they lost so many pieces of their costumes. It was a comforting thought that they weren't just litter filling up a gutter or a landfill somewhere, but part of an actual living creature. Their familiarity meant that they knew not any costume piece would do. It had to be something uncommon; nothing mass produced or popular, left behind because of abundance rather than being repulsive. It took a considerable amount of digging, but eventually Sam found what they were looking for.

"What are they?" David inquired.

"They're... gloves," assessed Sam. "And I think they're supposed to look like human hands?"

"That's ridiculous," Beth laughed. "What costume would call for that where you couldn't just use your own hands?" There was no tag or label on the silicone digits, just a plastic wire holding them together.

"It was probably some kind of cartoon character with a very distinct look. The company likely just made a costume based on an image without thinking about practicality. These are perfect. Hey Phil, how much?"

"If they don't have a price tag, you can probably just take them. I won't tell if you don't."

The next rhyme was already materializing on the scroll by the time they left the store. 'The hearts of killers hold great power. Vicious foes that make you cower. From those that possess threats beneath, bring back hair, or blood, or teeth.'

"...whoa," was all Beth could think to say. "I think I get what it's asking for, but where are we supposed to find something like that?"

"Do either of you happen to be a serial killer?" Sam laughed uncomfortably.

"Darn, no," Beth said sarcastically.

"I think I'm getting a headache..." David moaned faintly.

"Oh geez." Beth immediately ran to her brother's side and led him to a curb to sit on. "Sam, ask the scroll for the next item."

"But the Gamesman—"

"We don't really have a choice. There's only so much time left, and we're less than halfway done." She turned to her brother. "Just take it easy, buddy. You've probably just had a long night."

"...I know, Beth." There was a graveness in David's voice which caught his sister off guard. She looked at him and studied his face carefully. Something was very wrong.

"What do you mean, you know?"

"I know why my head hurts all the time, and I know why it's so important to Mom and Dad that I have a good Halloween."

"David..."

"I'm sick, right? That's what Death was about to say back in the graveyard? Don't make up some excuse or tell me I'm wrong. I hate how everyone keeps lying to me!"

"David, I..." Beth began to cry, and so did her brother. "How could you possibly know that? We've all been so careful."

"I just do."

"It's... do you remember this past summer when the headaches first started? Mom took you to a doctor and they scanned your head with a big sci-fi machine?"

"Yeah, Mom said they didn't find anything. But that wasn't true, was it?"

"They weren't sure what to call it," Beth explained with shaky breath. "A growth, I guess."

"So that explains it."

"Mom and Dad talked to three different doctors, and they all agreed there was no way to— wait, what did you just say?"

"Nothing."

"David."

"Okay, I have a secret too. I guess that makes us even. Ever since last summer, I can kind of..."

"What?"

"Hear people's thoughts? Not all the time, just when I really focus. Or if I'm not focused enough. The thing in my head could be what causes it.

Something like that happened to a guy in one of my comic books." David waited for his sister to say something. "You don't believe me?"

"Believe it or not," said Beth, her eyes wide and filled with contemplation, "I think I do. We've seen some wild stuff tonight. And it almost makes too much sense. That's how you knew about Dad burying the raccoon, or how you figured out what number the Gamesman was thinking of. Or—"

"You don't have to say it, sis. I know I'm dying."

Hearing her brother say it so plainly sent a wave of dread through Beth's body. She shot to her feet with a hand clasped over her mouth. Sam, who had been listening just a few feet away, went to comfort her, but she put a hand up to stop them.

"I'm fine," she muttered after a few deep breaths. "David, I'm so sorry."

"It's okay. We should win this contest."

"Speaking of," Sam spoke up. "I may actually have some good news. Listen to this. 'Death eternal comes to all. We have our time and then we fall. By the bright October moon, find a soul that's falling soon.'"

"That's me!" David exclaimed, a little too chipper for Beth or Sam's comfort, given what they had just been talking about. "Now there's just one other thing to get."

"Plus something from a killer," Beth reminded them.

"Yeah," said Sam. "That's the bad news. It looks like Gamesman skipped ahead to the end. We know the last item."

"What's the rhyme?" asked David.

"There is no rhyme. Just three words in extra thick letters: 'Spirit. Of. Halloween.'"

The trio arrived back in the graveyard just as the hour was coming to a close. The Gamesman was already there waiting for them.

"Slow going, kids?" he asked. "I got here first, so you may as well throw in the towel."

"It wasn't who could do it first," Sam reminded him. "Just, 'whoever most superbly carries out their task.'"

"Where do you like to be hit the least?" Beth asked the Gamesman.

"Why on Earth would I tell you that?"

"It's his shin!" David shouted excitedly. In the time it took him to regard David with a look of frustrated surprise, Beth smiled and delivered a swift kick as hard as she possibly could into the Gamesman's left shin.

"You miserable brats!" wailed their opponent. The way he hopped up and down while holding his bruised leg gave them all a solid chuckle.

"That's for my brother's eye, you piece of garbage."

"Well played, Beth Willows," whispered the Violent Dark. If their entrance before had been comparable to a lumbering rhino, now the gods of Halloween arrived with the stealth of a field mouse. In the place of Death was a woman who looked to be in her late twenties. She had unnaturally dark blue eyes, and raven hair tied in a Dutch braid over her right shoulder.

"Who are you?" asked Sam.

"Do you not recognize me, Sammy Haynes?" asked the woman. "I suppose that's a privilege, to say you can't recognize Death when it stands before you."

"You looked different last time..."

"I'm a certainty with many faces," said Death. "Very rarely do I look the same as I once did, although I have a couple favorites."

"Halloween is almost over!" bawled the thing called Garb. "Let us carry on with the results of the competition! The Gamesman arrived back here first, so he shall present his findings before the children."

"What treat have you brought me, Gamesman?" chirped the witch.

"A true rarity," boasted the foppishly-dressed villain. From out of his pocket, he produced a small piece of tinfoil. "Found only in Whisper Falls, made and distributed only ever on one night. Sarah Swete, I give you the candy which brought this town to its knees: Halloween Surprise!" Underneath the foil was something not quite chocolate or candy. Its surface was slick and coated in what looked like glassy sugar. The whole thing was shaped like a twenty-sided die.

"Oooooo! Gamesman, where did you find it? I thought they were all eaten or destroyed?"

"That detestable shopkeep owed me a favor."

"And you, children? What goodies do you have for your dear friend Sarah?"

Beth walked up to her and presented the peppermint twist in the little baggy Mrs. McCready had given them.

"Christmas candy?!" the witch wailed. "So rarely do I get to sample the treats of our sister holiday! Well done, children. Well done indeed!"

And what of my offering?" demanded Garb.

"That… is one thing I could not acquire," the Gamesman admitted. "Children, show us whatever attempt you've made, which is sure to pale in comparison even to the nothing I have brought."

"These gloves," said Sam. "Worthless to any human wearer." The thing called Garb trundled over towards them. Whenever it moved, it made a sound akin to a bike tire deflating. It stretched out an appendage made of stethoscopes and clown shoes and a few superhero masks, with a pair of novelty glasses on the end bearing a fake nose and eyebrows. Somehow that rubber nose sniffed the gloves Sam had put up, and then the individual pieces of the appendage spread apart until it grabbed them and gobbled them up.

"Your offering is acceptable to Garb."

"You're losing, Gamesman," growled the Violent Dark. "Can you redeem yourself, even in this small, trivial way, by bringing me the essence of a killer?"

"Easily," he boasted before pulling out a few of his own hairs. "I've taken plenty of lives, both literally and figuratively. This should more than suffice."

"Correct only by a technicality, worm. And what about you, children?"

"We... don't have anything," Beth frowned.

"Really, then why do I smell violence on you? Particularly from that one." The Violent Dark pointed to David.

"Oh my gosh!" David cried out. "We're so stupid. We had something all along." He ran his hands over the length of his costume, and produced a small tuft of black and brown hairs. "Bear's fur!"

"I don't believe it," Beth snorted.

"And the kill is fresh, too." A withered hand reached out from under the Violent Dark's robes and took the dog fur. "This will do nicely. Your move, Gamesman."

"Right. Something close to death, hmm? I've provided nicely. Come out now, you worthless pile of human and societal decay!" From out of the shadows came a man whose face was more stubble than skin. He wore a dirty gray hoodie that had some kind of logo or institution name on the front that had long since faded. His pants were filthy and torn in several places. "Chester here was happy to play me for the possibility of a hot meal. Sadly, he didn't have what it takes. All it cost him was the remaining years of his life, save for one half-hour. When you can't find what you need in stores, make your own; that's what Momma used to say, at least."

"You're despicable," Beth sneered.

"Yes, and you sound like Daffy Duck. What's your point?"

"Oh, you poor thing," said Death. She approached Chester and took one of his hands in both of hers. The homeless man looked both grateful and surprised to receive a kind touch. "What's he done to you?"

"I don't feel so well, ma'am."

"I'm sure you don't. Let's fix that. Would you come with me, please?" She led the man out into the graveyard, the pair disappearing in the fog. When she came back, Death was alone.

"You're not going to take my little brother, are you?" Beth asked anxiously.

"Only when it's his time, dear," said the woman, whose dark eyes Beth found surprisingly kind. "His time is soon, but not tonight. You've fulfilled your task, though, by bringing him here. That just leaves Spirit's assignment." All four of the gods looked to the scarecrow, who was still and imposing.

"I've brought this," said the Gamesman. From behind a tombstone, he revealed a jack-o'-lantern. Its eyes were exquisite triangles, carved so as to look like they were three dimensional. The mouth was a jagged, asymmetrical lightning bolt, looking nothing like the mouth of any creature, but nevertheless seeming as if it could begin laughing at any moment. "The most expertly-carved pumpkin in Whisper Falls, a contender for the best in this entire hemisphere. The chief symbol of the holiday, raised above all others like it."

"Very nice, Gamesman," spoke Death. "Beth, what does your group have?"

"We don't have anything like that."

"Then that's four to four!" chortled the Gamesman. "In my business, we call that a tie!"

"What happens in the event of a tie?" Sam asked.

"Spirit decides," said the Violent Dark.

"We heed his judgment," Garb exclaimed.

"Feel that wind blowing?" Sarah laughed. "He's rendering his verdict now!"

"A verdict has been reached," Death announced. "Each party shall be given a chance to make up for their failed task. Gamesman, would you part with your golden coat, your costume, of sorts, to the conglomerate Garb?"

"You're crazy," scoffed the Gamesman. "This jacket is the source of my powers!"

"A small price to pay for your freedom, no?"

"No!"

"Very well. Beth—"

"Wait!" the Gamesman tried to argue.

"David. Sam. If any of you can offer up the true spirit of Halloween, you win this contest, and with it, everything you've been promised."

"I think I can try," David said. He approached the gods, showing no hint of the fear he felt. "Halloween is supposed to be a time where you're allowed to be frightened. But I've been terrified for months now. Not by Halloween, but by what comes after. I'm not sleeping right, food doesn't taste as good as it used to, and it's hard to play with my friends now because it feels wrong.

"But, despite all that, despite how scared I am right now, I'm having a great time tonight. Because of Beth, and Sam, and even because of the Gamesman, in a weird sort of way. Isn't that what Halloween is, having a great time even while you're scared out of your pants?"

There was a moment of silence. Not total silence; the cars in the distance wouldn't stop for anything, but the wind held its breath, and every cricket had ceased their song as the entire graveyard waited for an answer. After almost a full minute, a big fat bag of candy dropped down beside David with a 'plunk.'

"No..." moaned the Gamesman.

"Congratulations," beamed Death. "Your team has won with a five-to-four lead."

"This can't be finished!" The Gamesman dropped to his knees. "I've done so much work for you!"

"Your contribution to the debt is nil!" chided Garb.

"Better luck next year, dearie," Sarah Sweet giggled.

"Hold on!" David called out.

"What are you doing, bud?" asked Beth, who only seconds ago had been relieved to get to go home.

"Gamesman, I'll play you in a double or nothing," said the young boy, before looking to Spirit for permission.

"We will not grant the Gamesman a favor," said the Violent Dark. "But you may wager the remainder of your winnings if you so choose."

"I don't know what you're getting at, boy, but I have nothing to put up. You've taken everything from me!"

"What about the source of your powers?"

"Your comprehension skills really are dismal, aren't they?" the Gamesman laughed. "You just witnessed me refuse to gamble that!"

"I'll bet something else too. Since you're offering the source of your powers, I'll offer the source of mine." This caught the Gamesman's attention.

"So, you *do* possess abilities!" he whooped. "I knew you couldn't have beaten me fairly."

"Like your games were ever fair. Do we have a bet?"

"Freedom and power," mused the Gamesman. "Much better than just freedom. Alright, I accept. I've been at this long enough that I can tell you have a game in mind, so hurry up and name it."

"Staring contest, we start now." The two foes looked into each other's eyes, David's small and meek, and the Gamesman's yellow and sinister.

And then David blinked.

The Gamesman staggered backward, as both David's power and the sensation of his burden being lifted all hit him at once.

"It's so… noisy," he muttered.

"You might figure that out," David teased. "Congratulations, you can read people's thoughts now."

"David…" Beth gasped. "What did you just do?"

"Spirit gave me the idea."

"You can understand him?" Sam asked in disbelief.

"You can understand him?" Death parroted.

"Well, not anymore."

"What did that… *thing* tell you to do to me?"

"Exactly what I said," laughed David. "Gave you the source of my power, which just so happened to be a gross thing in my brain."

"You're lying!" the Gamesman shrieked, pointing an accusatory finger at the boy.

"Nope, you can ask Spirit yourself now."

The Gamesman turned with a look of growing horror towards Spirit O'Halloween. First his eyes widened, and then his mouth hung open. Whatever thoughts he saw or heard, it brought out a bone-chilling scream from deep in the pit of his stomach. He tripped over his own legs as he tried to get away, and when he finally got moving, he flipped over a tombstone and rolled right back into a sprint.

"David!" called Beth. She ran over and wrapped her arms around her brother's neck in the biggest hug she could muster. "I can't believe you just did that! How do you feel?"

"No more headache! I... I feel good."

"This is crazy." Beth allowed herself to cry for the second time tonight, but the emotions behind these tears were completely new.

"Shouldn't one of you go after the Gamesman?" Sam asked the gods of Halloween.

"He and I will meet again before long," Death sighed.

"He has his freedom," said the Violent Dark. "Now he's free to die."

"A real shame," sobbed Sarah Swete. "He was fun to play with."

"Good riddance," groaned Garb.

"Did the plan really work?" David asked them. "Am I cured?"

"Let me put it this way," Death chuckled. "You forfeited your right to ask us for a favor of your choosing, but we can still grant you a boon. Not everyone chooses to let the spirit of Halloween into their hearts, with many losing it as they grow older. To them, October 31st just becomes another day. The three of you, though, for as long as you continue to choose the tenets of Halloween, the sweetness and the scares, the darkness and the light, you'll never have a bad Halloween for as long as you live. And David?"

"Yes?"

"You have many Halloweens ahead of you. Cherish them well."

Carol of the Falls

"Bart, I don't want to alarm you, but there may be a Boogeyman or BoogeyMEN in the house!" –
Homer Simpson (1993)

The Boogeyman is gonna get you.

That phrase had haunted Ralph Dyniaski for most of his childhood. It wasn't the threat itself which bothered him, but the vagueness of it. 'Get you' could mean just about anything. Get you like in a game of tag? Get you like a parent gets you home from school? Get you after a long chase, to punish or to harm? That last one unnerved Ralph the most; he had just enough awareness of the things that went beyond harm to make his skin crawl.

His familiarity with the phrase, and subsequent phobia of the Boogeyman, started on the night of October 31st, three years prior. A group of older boys surrounded Ralph and his friends and began chanting it over and over again, which sent him running home crying in fear. It was two whole days before Ralph realized that he had no idea what the statement actually meant, but the incident had left a psychological scar. The following Christmas, Ralph's uncle Mike began to tease him about the coming of Krampus. When he described the creature as "just a sort of boogeyman," it sent the boy into a conniption.

But Ralph was ten now, and determined to become the master of his own destiny. To do so, he began his quest in the same place many do to attain such a status: the library.

It wasn't easy at first. The public library nearest to Ralph's house, being a small, local branch, did not have a dedicated section on the Boogeyman, or even 'boogeymen.' Ralph tried to ask the head librarian for assistance, but he had a hard time explaining to Ms.

Nightshade exactly what he was looking for. He wound up being directed to the fiction section, filled with dog-eared horror novellas and pulp thrillers, some of which were even older than Ralph's parents, and all of which were relatively useless to him. Having to ask someone multiple times for help with the same problem made Ralph anxious, but given the intent of his research was to lessen his fears, he fought past the malaise and reframed his request.

"You could try mythology," said Ms. Nightshade.

"Isn't that just more fiction?" Ralph asked.

"Sort of. But there's historical context too, cultural implications. They could tell you more than your typical work of King or Koontz. Your Boogeyman might just be hiding in the pages of one of those books." When the boy rubbed his arm uncomfortably, she added, "and no, Ralph, I don't mean literally."

The books Ralph found during his second go were admittedly more relevant to his interests, but nothing specifically jumped out at him. He needed something tangible and specific, a text that could spell out a solution to his problem; make the Boogeyman less of a specter in his life and more of a subject. He had already wasted much of his Saturday on this errand, though, and he was getting bored.

While taking a seat against a stack of books, Ralph leaned back on his palms, nearly falling when the feel of cobwebs and dust made him shoot up off the floor. If not for that moment of disgust, the boy may not have noticed there was a book encased in all that grime, lodged between a leg of the shelf and the wall. Not yet tired enough to lose his sense of curiosity,

Ralph liberated it from the ground and blew away the dust, the way he'd seen protagonists of countless children's films do with ancient tomes.

Golden, inlaid letters spelled out 'Folklore and Urban Legends of Whisper Falls' on the cover. The book itself was covered front to back in engravings that Ralph reckoned were supposed to be vines, but he thought they looked more like veins. They reminded him of the kind that appeared on a book of nursery rhymes Ralph's grandparents read to him when he was younger, although those depicted characters like Humpty Dumpty and Little Boy Blue, who had been repeatedly etched on paper using Ralph's crayons. While these were much different, they felt familiar all the same, which compelled the boy to crack open the text, regardless of what it might offer him.

Inside were a number of entries which could have captivated Ralph for hours, titles like 'The Woman in the Waterfall,' or 'Creeping Charlie.' 'The Secret Language of Statues' was one that particularly appealed to him, but he was on a mission, so he forced himself to focus. A half-formed memory came back from English class, and Ralph flipped to the back of the book looking for an index. These pages looked more faded than the rest of the book, but miraculously, there under the B's was the word he was looking for, one that filled the boy with dread: Boogeyman. The text said to 'see 'Carol of the Falls' page 23.' Ralph did as he was told.

The passage described an old tradition celebrated in Whisper Falls: Halloween caroling. Ralph had never thought to question why Christmas caroling was so common, but the same thing wasn't done in October. It seemed so obvious, which made him eager to learn more. The premise was simple: rather than the standard 'trick-or-treat,' a Halloween caroler sings a song after knocking on someone's door, and for their efforts they receive greater treats than they would otherwise.

There is a catch, though. According to the book, somewhere in Whisper Falls waits 'the Caroler,' and if the Caroler hears your song, they will attempt to get you. The phrasing of that part gave Ralph pause. It was too vague; 'get you.' He was on the right track.

From there, any trick-or-treaters who had been singing must race home before the Caroler catches up with them. If they make it, they are safe and free to enjoy the sweet spoils of October. It never elaborated on what happened if the Caroler got you, or even what determined who the Caroler was. What it did provide, though, was an example of a standard Halloween carol. Ralph studied the lyrics carefully:

We monsters of the Underworld are out in search of treats.
We fill the air with shrieks and howls, and sounds of stomping feet.
Our path is made through stygian night, and across the River Styx.
So fill our bags, you fools and hags, or else you'll get our tricks.
If caroling should be a sin, may Hell be where we go.
Though on the way, we must delay; the Caroler's out, you know.
Before too long, our festive song, will draw him out, and then,
The blackest night in Whisper Falls will soon begin again.
If we should meet the Caroler, don't ask us where we'll be.

We'll move our bones towards our homes, and after that, we're free.
If we don't, he'll hunt us down, wearing the widest grin.
And if he makes it to your house, you mustn't let him in.

There were more lyrics, but they were further down the page from the rest of the song, and something about the font seemed strange to Ralph. It looked as if whoever wrote them down, since the song was photocopied from a hand-written page, had been pressing a lot harder with their pen, like something had spooked them good while they were writing. It sent a chill up Ralph's spine to think about, although the lyrics themselves didn't help:

You must not let the Caroler in, use sword, or spear, or flame.
He'll crawl inside, you'll wish you died. He'll make you both the same.
Do not let the Caroler in, on this don't break or bend,
Or else he'll make you know his mask, and get you in the end.

There it was again, 'get you.' The rest of the passage was only more disturbing. It went on to explain that the 'blackest night in Whisper Falls' mentioned in the song referred to the origins of the tradition. The first Caroler was actually a serial killer who lived in Whisper Falls a long time ago, someone who killed anywhere between thirteen and twenty-three people. It was long enough ago that the details became fuzzy, including the true identity of the killer. They were just the Caroler now, a 'boogeyman' who sang songs on Halloween to get invited into people's homes, and once they were inside, they struck.

An older girl at school named Rhonda Dougherty had once told Ralph that a lot of Halloween traditions, especially things like wearing costumes and giving out candy, were originally started as a way of appeasing the dead. It made sense to Ralph, then, when the book explained that people in Whisper Falls had begun 'Halloween caroling' as a way of paying tribute to the Caroler's victims. And really, didn't it make sense that a community would want to put that awful night behind them? Associate the idea with a fun game instead of a tragedy?

Ralph desperately wanted to take the book home, but Ms. Nightshade said no. Something about it not having an ISBN number, which was very odd. Then why was it in the library at all? The librarian couldn't give him an answer, which meant he would have to sell the concept to his friends at school tomorrow without a visual aid.

He was careful about how he framed it. Though he had put in a lot of effort to convince his classmates that he wasn't a crybaby coward who was afraid of the Boogeyman, the truth was that the harder kids pushed back against such labels, the more it validated them to their peers. So, he downplayed the role that the Caroler played in the ritual, emphasizing the veritable mountains of candy they would receive. To Ralph's surprise, however, his friends liked the story better with a monster in it.

"I bet he uses a chainsaw," said Nathan Mancuso. "All the best killers use chainsaws."

“Nuh-uh,” argued Ryan Williams. “Kitchen knife, easily. Or a big metal needle.”

“Maybe the Caroler just pretends to be scary for a minute and then lets us go,” whimpered Leslie Mancuso, Nathan’s twin sister, who was the only one in their friend group considered just as timid as Ralph was.

They debated the merits of Ralph’s idea for most of their lunch period. Eventually there were six kids interested in joining Ralph on Halloween for a bout of caroling. It was Warren Vallier, Ralph’s best friend, who sealed the deal.

“Ralph thought of it,” said Warren, “so he should take point. What are you thinking, Ralphie?”

“Oh, um...” Ralph hadn’t expected to be put on the spot like this. He took a couple pieces of crumpled paper out of his pocket and smoothed them out. One had a list of notes he had made at the library.

“So, we should pick costumes that we can move in and aren’t too heavy. We don’t want to get tired and give up halfway through.” Everyone nodded their agreement. “And forget plastic pails shaped like jack-o’-lanterns or little sacks with a ghost or a vampire on them. We’re expecting lots of candy, so everyone grab garbage bags from home. And does anybody have a wagon? It would be helpful to have a wagon to carry our stuff.”

“I have a wagon,” said Leslie.

“Perfect,” Ralph said before gesturing to the second paper. “I also copied this map of Whisper

Falls. I think I have a good route planned out that will keep us from wasting too much time."

"We can't go this way," said Warren, tracing Stine Street on the map with his finger. There's construction, so a lot of the sidewalk is gone. And we should avoid Ashley Street; it's a hill that ends in a dead end; not good for what we're planning at all."

Ralph nodded and started erasing lines. They met after school to finalize their path before heading home. Ralph and Warren lived in the same neighborhood, so they usually walked together.

"What's your costume gonna be, Ralphie?"

Ralph stopped in his tracks and stared off into the middle distance.

"You didn't think of one, did ya?" Warren chuckled.

"I planned so much!" Ralph exclaimed. "I guess I forgot about step one: pick a costume!"

"That's okay," said Warren. "I thought of a few ideas. I'll let you have the best one, though."

"Really? You would do that for me?"

"Sure, we're pals. So, you ready to hear it?"

Ralph smiled the widest grin and nodded. "I'm ready."

"Baseball player."

"That's not really scary..."

"Ralphie, Ralphie. You need to consider the brilliance of what I'm telling you. What does a baseball player do when they hit a ball over the back fence?"

"They run home?"

"Exactly. And what are we supposed to do if we find the Caroler?"

"...run home!" Ralph shouted happily.

"Bingo, bongo. The costume is super simple, so it won't slow you down, and the pants are designed for running. And the best part: it gives you an excuse to carry a bat."

"Why does that matter?"

"Well, you gotta defend yourself if the Caroler catches up, right?"

"What, with the bat?!" Ralph had seldom ever thought about hitting a baseball with a baseball bat, much less a person. "I dunno... couldn't I really hurt someone that way?"

"You want the Caroler to hurt you instead?"

"No..."

"Then you gotta be prepared to do what you gotta do," said Warren, sounding deadly serious. "Think on it, will ya?"

Ralph thought about it long after they parted ways. It kept him up at night in the week leading up to Halloween. Ultimately, he did ask his mom to make him a baseball jersey, although he still wasn't sure if he could attack someone, even if it was the Boogeyman...

When the seven of them met on the 31st, Ralph was really optimistic about their candy chances. The Mancusos brought a wagon, as promised. They were dressed as salt and pepper shakers, wearing gray and white shirts respectively with large name tags on their chests, and chrome cooking pots on their heads that completed the look.

Michael Dacosta, who was dressed as a devil, brought a whole box of garbage bags from home, ensuring they had extras. Ryan Williams, an avid fan of conspiracy theories and sci-fi movies, was dressed as a green alien with a ray gun in hand and an antenna on top of his head. Laurie Dubois was a colorful clown adorned in reds, yellows, and blues, with pale white makeup on her face and a puffy red wig on top of her head.

Warren's costume was the best, though. An imposing werewolf, with a domino-style mask that had fake fur, an unnaturally large, furrowed brow, and fangs stretching out from the underside. He wore a ratty plaid button-up that was cut to look like something had expanded in size inside it. Human hair was glued on the backs of his hand, which featured claws for fingernails.

"One of my sisters made them for me," Warren explained. "They're an old set of press-on nails she had lying around. She filed the ends and painted them so they'd look like real claws."

"That's so clever!" said Leslie.

"Are they uncomfortable?" Ralph asked.

"A little," Warren winced. "They're glued on real good. Might lose a nail or two trying to get them off later."

When they got to their first house, no one was brave enough to act. None of them dared say "trick-or-treat"; there was an unspoken understanding that if they did that, they would be disqualifying themselves from the act of caroling by assuming the role of garden-variety candy seekers. It was Warren the Werewolf who stepped up first, stumbling over the first few lines of the song Ralph had given them all copies of.

Ralph soon joined in, emboldened by his friend's initiative, and by the time they were all at it, they sounded like a proper merry band. There was an awkward silence afterwards, and Ralph began to worry that he had been sold a lie by a very old book, but then the couple at the door laughed so hard that they nearly fell over, clapping their hands in delight and pouring two bowls of candy and chips into their bags. Everyone looked at each other with overjoyed disbelief before shouting rushed thank-yous and hurrying to the next house.

Their song was a hit. Everywhere they went, people responded to their singing like it was magic. Older couples were especially susceptible, it seemed. Barb and Ivan Callaghan said they could remember Halloween caroling over fifty years ago, before distributing two full-sized chocolate bars per head, more than the standard one each. The Cooneys gave out lollipops, the bulbous kind that no child with even a shred of sense dared bite into for fear of shattering their teeth. The Spearins, whose family owned Whisper Falls' largest movie theater, had bags of their signature popcorn, which they gave out in excessive numbers. And the Butterworths had chocolate coins, which the group got enough of that they could have retired at ten years old if it were real currency.

After just half an hour of caroling, they were filthy with sweet and salty treats. The wagon's wheels groaned under the weight of three full trash bags, which the group had started putting half of their take into for a communal allotment. This kept their own bags from filling up too quickly, although even those were getting difficult to hold closed.

"Hey, Ryan," said Nathan. "I'm getting tired over here. You have a spaceship we can carry this stuff in?"

"For the ninth time, no," Ryan huffed.

"My arms are starting to hurt," Laurie concurred.

"Maybe we should quit while we're ahead?" suggested Michael.

"Let's leave it up to our fearless leader," said Warren. "How 'bout it, Ralph?"

"Wait, I'm the leader?" gasped the dumbfounded baseball player.

"This whole thing was your idea," Warren pointed out.

"Yeah!" Leslie agreed. "And it worked out great! We won't need to spend our allowance on snacks again until the new year!"

Ralph was someone who got scared easily, it was true, but being easily frightened could let in fear's more insidious sibling: worry. Worry was a different animal than fear. They were closely linked, yes, but worry had a tendency to sneak its way into all kinds of places. Worry could make a person believe that nothing would ever work out the way they wanted, that the worst things that could happen probably would. So, even though things had gone extraordinarily well, all the way from when Ralph first proposed the idea to the present moment, it hadn't really dawned on Ralph that this was the case.

And it wasn't just being singled out as the leader that did it (though, that was nice too); it was the 'fearless' part. Tonight, he wasn't Ralph the scaredy cat, or Ralph the crybaby, or Ralph the worrywart. He was Ralph Dyniaski, the fearless leader, and that felt good. He regarded the wagon, figuring that if they ate a little bit of their candy along the way, they could fit one more garbage bag on it.

"Let's go a little further."

They hit a few more houses along Price Street. Excitement grew among them when they got to the home of Randall Pitty, a recently retired ice cream man who usually went all out for Halloween, less so in the last couple years since his wife had passed away. But even if his house only had one paltry jack-o'-lantern on the porch and an ancient paper skeleton on the door, they just knew he'd still have good candy.

"Well, who's all this, then?" Mr. Pitty said with a big smile after opening the door. "I see Ralph Dyniaski, and Laurie Dubois. And is that Warren Vallier under that werewolf mask?"

"Guilty, sir," Warren tittered.

Mr. Pitty took the time to greet each of the kids by name, remembering some of his best customers from summers past. It made them feel important; special, like they were people and not just 'kids.'

"Alright," said Pitty. "I've got a whole mess of chocolate peanut butter cups that are no good to me and my diabetes, but I can't give 'em to ya until I hear those magic words."

They sang with their whole chests. It was a routine now; gone was the timidness of youth that came with doing something silly in front of other people for the first time. It helped that everyone who had seen them do it thus far had responded with unconditional praise. Mr. Pitty, though... he just stared at them blankly.

"Uh... Everything okay, Mr. P?" said Warren.

It was as if Randall Pitty had been teetering on a precipice, and the werewolf's words finally pushed him over. He dropped the bowl of peanut butter cups, which crashed on the concrete porch with surprising force, before staggering backwards and catching himself on the wall. His other hand clutched madly at his heart.

Everyone took a step forward to help before stopping. Much like vampires, they hesitated to enter someone else's home without express permission. Mr. Pitty's eyes were sharp and unfocused, not looking at anything in particular. His breathing was abnormally regular, like someone imitating healthy respiration as opposed to coming by it naturally.

"A-Are you alright, sir?" Ralph asked.

"Oh," said Pitty, stretching out the single syllable. "I'll be fine. Just remembering what it's like to feel again."

And then he punched the wall to his right so hard that it cracked.

He hit it again and again, harder each time, never turning away from the group. Leslie shrieked, and Ryan covered his eyes like it would erase the act. After more than a dozen strikes, there was a mangled hole in the drywall around Pitty's bloody fist.

"Pain," he said casually, reaching his arm into the wall and rooting around for something. "I remember that one. Plentiful, made to be shared." When the arm came out, it held something small and made from wood. A mask.

"You should go to the hospital..." said Michael. "Can we use your phone? One of us can call for the ambulance."

"None of us are going to need an ambulance," said Pitty, placing the mask over his face. It was some crude mix of a tiger and a wolf, carved from ancient-looking driftwood and covered in a layer of dust and plaster. Despite the simplicity of its design, it bore an expression that struck Ralph as almost... mean. Like it was the cruelest, most hateful thing to ever walk the Earth.

"Not me," Pitty continued, "and certainly not you. There'd be no point. By the time the ambulance got to you, it would be far, far too late."

Everyone's blood ran cold. No one knew what to think about what they just heard. They were afraid, sure, but it was a fear like seeing a typically kind teacher have to yell at their class, or the kind of anxiety that came from knowing you were about to get in trouble for something you were definitely guilty of. It wasn't terror, that primal, bone-chilling horror that robbed a person of their reason, reason that reminded them that Mr. Pitty was acting peculiarly, sure, but not so much so that they had anything to actually worry about. Yet that was how they each reacted when Mr. Pitty took his first step towards them through the doorway.

They screamed. They screamed so loud that several neighborhood dogs began a chorus of barking. The wind howled especially wild and perniciously, like it sympathized with the sensation but took pleasure in bearing witness to it all the same.

And then they ran. None of them dared look back at first; no one was eager to confirm what they knew in their hysteric hearts to be true: they were being followed. It wasn't until they reached the end of Price Street that anyone spoke again.

"What the heck is happening?!" wailed Nathan.

Ralph was about to answer before Warren said, "it's the Caroler. We woke him up!"

"We're all going to die!" Ryan cried.

"Keep it together!" They all looked to Warren. "We just have to make it back home. That's what the song says, right?"

"That's just a stupid song," moaned Laurie. "It doesn't mean it's true!"

"The part about there being a Caroler was true," Warren pointed out. "Why shouldn't the part about being able to make it home safe be true as well?"

Ralph was grateful to have Warren here. He would have said the same things to the group, but he wasn't sure he'd have been able to do it without crying. He wasn't sure he wasn't crying right now. Not wanting the group to see his face either way, he risked a look back.

"Um, guys?"

The Caroler was indeed still following them. But while they had been booking it back the way they came as fast as they could move, the Caroler seemed to just be having a casual saunter down the street. How was he keeping pace with them?

Laurie screamed again when the group saw what Ralph was seeing.

"Don't focus on that," instructed Warren. "He likes Halloween songs? Let's give him some of our own! Who wants to start?"

"Monster Mash!"

"Thriller!"

"Spooky Scary Skeletons!"

Warren meant for them to actually sing one of these songs, but the group got preoccupied with simply naming as many Halloween songs as they could think of. It worked just as well, keeping them focused on their game rather than the fact that their legs ached and their lungs burned, or that both those things threatened to serve them to the Caroler if they slowed down even a little.

Michael's house was the closest. "Good luck," he said in half a breath as he ran up the path to his front door. They lost Laurie next, although no one was sure if they actually saw her turn off towards her street. She had been falling behind, her clown costume too baggy to run comfortably in. Everyone silently decided that she had made it home, and that they would see her at school on Monday. The alternative was something they weren't ready to contend with.

"We better get on the news for this," huffed Ryan as he turned towards his parents' apartment complex.

They were down to four, and Salt and Pepper were falling behind.

"Pick up the pace, Nathan!" Warren shouted.

"Leslie, he's gaining on us!" screamed Ralph.

"It's this stupid wagon slowing us down," Nathan groaned.

"Lose it!" commanded Warren.

"But..." Leslie whimpered. "We got this wagon for Christmas last year!"

"Good thing Christmas is just a couple months away, huh?"

"He's right, sis." Nathan took the wagon handle and sent it careening down a hill towards a playground, where it hit a seesaw before flipping over with a distant metallic thud. The wagon's cargo was launched further, exploding like a sad piñata.

"We can go back first thing tomorrow," Ralph said, trying to comfort the forlorn twins. "I bet the wagon will still be there."

They ran further and faster, and the entire time, the Caroler in his driftwood mask kept pace with them while never running himself.

"I'm going to try something," Warren said before stopping so abruptly that his shoes left skid marks on the pavement.

"What are you doing?" Leslie hissed.

"We have to go!" stammered Ralph.

"I'm going to try fighting him." Warren brandished the claws on his hand. "I have three older sisters; I've seen them defend themselves with just their regular nails. Imagine what I can do with these babies!"

"But..." was all Ralph could say.

"We're close enough to my house that I can split off from here anyway. I'll scratch him up a bit and then go. Trust me, Ralphie, I'll be fine. Buy you guys some time to get home and enjoy your candy."

Ralph wanted to protest further, but he trusted his friend and didn't want to be a crybaby anymore, so he just nodded with a stiff upper lip. "Come on, you guys," he said to Nathan and Leslie. They never looked back, but Ralph did hear the sound of a werewolf howling behind them.

Nathan and Leslie got home safe. "Are you going to be okay, dude?" Nathan asked before they went inside.

"I think so," said Ralph, looking over his shoulder. "We haven't seen the Caroler in a little bit. Maybe Warren got him."

"Yeah, maybe," was all Nathan said before heading inside. Leslie gave a sympathetic smile and wave, following her brother without another word.

Ralph looked the way he was supposed to go to get home, and he felt a tired kind of unease coat his limbs. He was the only person outside, and the wind was whining and wailing. Before this game began, home was a tangible goal, just down a few streets and up a hill. Now, home was 'out there'; distant and alien, so far away on a night getting progressively colder and lonelier.

And then he heard the whistling.

Coming up an alleyway that cut between two neighborhoods was the Caroler, whistling a tune that seemed to match the song they had been singing all night. Warren was nowhere to be seen, and that made Ralph sick to his stomach.

In the heat of the moment, Ralph made a rash decision and started running a different way. There was a little area off in one corner of the neighborhood that everyone called 'the park,' but really it was just a small field with a few benches and an asphalt path down the middle. The treeline, however, backed onto the creek which ran through most of Whisper Falls, with a little bridge overtop that Ralph and his friends sometimes used as a shortcut to and from school. Ralph was sure that could get him home faster if he cut through a few yards after.

"Nearly over now!" called the Caroler, which only pushed Ralph to move even faster. The math he did in his head, not with exact numbers but hope and optimism only a desperate ten-year-old could conjure, told him that if he got across the creek, there was no way the Caroler could catch him. And then he got to the bridge, where his hopes were slayed completely.

A large metal gate had been erected in the middle of the bridge, with additional orange wire fencing and safety cones making the route even less accessible. An official sign from the municipality of Whisper Falls was on the front, citing 'structural issues' and 'other safety irregularities' as the reason for the barricade. Ralph pushed desperately at it, but it wouldn't budge. Realizing he'd be stuck on the bridge if the Caroler caught up to him now, he double-backed and took a hard left towards the creek.

The water was high, and the banks were steep. Ralph lost his footing and slid down the muddy embankment, barely keeping himself from falling. There were scattered rocks in the water. If he took his time and kept calm, he figured that he could hop across just fine. Problem was, he wasn't calm, and he didn't have time. He could try and just go for it, but the water looked terribly cold and was running awfully fast. Would the river be a kinder assassin than this mystery Caroler?

"You gave it your best shot, kid." Ralph's nerves froze. He could hear traces of Mr. Pitty's voice in the one that the Caroler spoke with, but not enough. Not nearly enough. "It doesn't change anything, but you gave me one helluva chase. So, any last words?"

"What are you?" Ralph turned around slowly, throwing his bag of candy into the river. He didn't think he'd be getting away, so there was no point in hoarding it now, but if there was even a slim chance, he couldn't have anything weighing him down.

"Excuse me?"

"I'm not stupid. I know Mr. Pitty wasn't secretly some crazy maniac all these years. So, if you're not him, what are you?"

"What an astute little boy you are."

"Answer the question!"

"Whoa, now..." the Caroler chuckled.

"I know what you are, but I want to hear you say it. I played your game; you owe me that much!"

"And what is it you think I am, Ralph Dyniaski?" The Caroler took a single step forward, and Ralph took a step back in response. His foot sank up to the ankle in wet mud.

"The... the Boogeyman!"

"Ha!" The Caroler began to laugh, and he didn't stop for almost a full minute. Ralph was paralyzed with fear, but he could feel water running into his shoe and up his pant leg. “I suppose I might be. You see, I’m so old, Ralph. Old enough that it’s hard to remember what I am or where I come from. But I’m pretty sure my father was the Violent Dark, and if the Boogeyman ever had a daddy, it was definitely him...”

“I don’t understand...”

The Caroler cocked his head to the side suddenly, fast enough that it startled Ralph horribly. “Are you scared of the Boogeyman, Ralphie?”

“N-No!”

“We’ll see.” The Caroler began to walk forward. “Can you scream for me, Ralph?”

“Stay away from me!” the boy shouted. His heart was pounding, and a cold sweat had bled through the entirety of his baseball cap.

“I love it when they scream...”

“I’m warning you...”

“Warren did.”

CRACK!

Ralph acted without thinking, taking the baseball bat and swinging it with all his might into the side of the Caroler’s head. The mask flew off his face and tumbled down into the river before disappearing. The man (or at least the thing pretending to be a man) went down, as Ralph’s dad would say, like a sack of potatoes.

The night was quiet. The only ones caroling now were the crickets and the frogs, and a distant owl hooting a duet with a humming streetlight. Ralph had knocked himself over with the force of his swing. Mud caked the entire right side of his body, and he held his breath. When the Caroler did not move after several minutes, Ralph slowly crawled his way over to the body. He had to be sure, had to be really sure that this nightmare was over.

He caught the faintest glimpse of Mr. Pitty's face, the blank eyes and the skull not in the shape it should be, and had to look away while he gagged. If the sight didn't make him throw up, the smell might. While he was distracted, the body jerked into motion, grabbing Ralph by both wrists and pinning him to the ground.

Ralph did scream this time. He wanted to call for help, but all he could do was make half-formed words with what little remained of his energy. It wouldn't have helped either way; there was no one around to hear him.

The Caroler's head hung limply, its eyes glazed over and glassy. Slowly its mouth came open, and a black spider the size of Ralph's palm crawled out. It was the ugliest spider Ralph had ever seen, all gnarled legs like tree branches and a body that looked like it was made from scrambled moss and half-digested licorice. Its nine eyes were beady and silver, reflecting what little moonlight there was, and it made a sound like a rattlesnake's tail, only slower.

It lowered itself down from the Caroler's mouth towards the boy's face on a web line, and Ralph screamed again. He screamed so forcefully that he was sure something inside him would burst. It only stopped when the spider crawled inside his mouth. The faltering logical part of Ralph's brain knew that no matter what this spider was, he could still bite it in half and it would be done. If he chewed it up and spit it out, it couldn't hurt him, but there was no way he could bring himself to do it. The thought of the spider's innards and guts, its juices and entrails, making contact with any part of his mouth... it offended a primal part of him that he couldn't fight.

He could feel the spider squirming in the back of his mouth, and when he couldn't scream anymore, the world went white.

Ralph woke up in his bed, sweat coating every fiber of his sheets. He would have been screaming if he weren't out of breath, so it came out more like a squeak that hurt his throat and made him cough. It took a while for the haze of sleep to leave his mind. Had it all been a dream? There was a muddy baseball player costume on his floor among his other dirty laundry, so it couldn't have been. But that meant...

Ralph rushed to the bathroom and splashed cold water on his face. He studied himself in the mirror closely, paying particular attention to his eyes for reasons he couldn't name. It looked like there was something there just behind his gaze, but whenever he tried to hone in on it, he couldn't look anymore.

When his parents asked him how his Halloween was, he simply said it was fine and couldn't say more, no matter how hard he tried. It was the same at school on Monday. No one from their group (which felt conspicuously smaller) said much about it that differed from any normal Halloween night, but Ralph wanted to say more. He just couldn't get the words out, though, whether it was by talking or writing them down; even alluding to what happened was impossible.

The weeks rolled on, Halloween quickly turning into Christmas, turning into New Years, turning into Valentine's Day. Ralph got less and less sure that his Halloween night had been anything out of the ordinary. That was, until certain times he was alone, where his mind was occupied doing things like chores or homework. Sometimes he would catch himself humming an unmistakable tune, and Ralph would start to cry.

The memory of that night faded from Ralph's mind by the following Halloween, but for the rest of his life, he'd never be without a certain sense of dread in the back of his thoughts, like a spider crawling on the inside of his skull. It happened especially the closer he got to October 31st, the dread that he'd hear someone else singing that song when they came to his door. Dread that he'd lose himself to havoc and violence clad in a driftwood mask. Dread that he was always that close to becoming the worst version of himself.

Dread, but never fear. Ralph never felt much in the way of fear ever again. He didn't have to; the thing he was afraid of most in the world had already happened to him.

The Boogeyman got him in the end.

What Happened to Ray Brady

"Monsters are real, and ghosts are real, too. They live inside us, and sometimes, they win." -Stephen King

Kevin Salt wandered into Whisper Falls at 6:45 in the morning on a Tuesday in October. He hadn't intended to come here. When he visited the bus depot two towns over the previous night, he simply looked for the most crowded vehicle with a sleep-deprived-looking driver that might not notice him sneaking on amidst the students and graveyard shifters. The trick didn't work every time, but it worked enough to still be an efficient way of getting around when you were a broke drifter.

This place had its own unique smell. Most cities did, Kevin found, at least for those who took the time to stop and smell the urbanity. Though there weren't any visible, he reasoned that the name 'Whisper Falls' must be at least partially literal, with one or several waterfalls being littered throughout, giving the place a wet and muggy scent that was distinct from places near a lake or ocean. This was blanketed by the wafting aromas of autumn; dead leaves, pumpkins both fresh and rotting, petrichor from a brief midnight rainfall.

To Kevin Salt, it smelled like opportunity. It may not have been his destination, but that didn't matter; Whisper Falls would work just as well as any other place. There was something calling out to him, and whatever it was led him here. He didn't know who, and he didn't know how, and he didn't know when, but there was one thing Kevin Salt was sure of:

He was going to kill somebody.

But this story isn't about Kevin Salt. It's about Ray Brady, aged eleven. At the time that Salt was plotting his dark deeds, Ray Brady was still asleep in his bed, blissfully unaware of serial killers and the other ugliness of the world.

In a lot of ways, Ray was just like any other kid. He liked playing softball in the summer, video games in the winter. In the spring he rode his bike, and in the fall he wore black and orange, the benevolent omen of Halloween casting happy shadows over his bright life. And like a lot of kids, Ray liked to think he was a lot more mature than he actually was. Ever since his age had hit double digits, he may as well have been an adult, according to no one but himself.

For the past several months (Ray could not have narrowed down the exact time period if you asked him) the Brady boy had been having dreams about someone he came to understand, somewhat childishly, was his imaginary friend, an enigmatic and playful character that called itself Mister Fox. Ray never saw Mister Fox, at least not completely. When they met, it was in an empty room filled with white mist, and crackling black static that was always just outside the boundaries of what Ray could touch. When Mister Fox felt close, the outlines of his big, yellow eyes and wide, toothy smile were just barely visible in the fog.

“It's a bit boring in here,” Ray had said after he'd gotten used to their meetings.

“Boring?!” replied Mister Fox in his powerful and raspy voice. “We're in an Imagination Room, one of the greatest places there is! It looks sparse now, but that's only to leave space for the things you can invent with your mind. How about it, Ray? What should we create?”

"A pirate ship could be fun?" Before Ray had even finished speaking, the dreamscape wove an entire seafaring scene around them. They were on a proper galleon, with four sails, a crow's nest, over a dozen cannons, and a loyal crew. Ray was the captain, and he could see Mister Fox now, or First Mate Fox, as he was called here, dressed like the finest pirate with a vulpine head Ray had ever witnessed. They had a bloody and exciting battle with a rival ship, and the dream ended as they were about to sail into a whirlpool towards their next adventure.

Ray had many adventures like this with Mister Fox; not always pirates, but always equally thrilling. It was easy for Ray to pull from the cartoons he watched or the books he read, but that strength quickly revealed a weakness in their little journeys into fantasy. It didn't matter how many giant robots Ray fought, or trips to the moon he and Mister Fox took; there were limits to his imagination that started to make these episodes feel hollow and unsatisfying.

"That is a pickle," said Mister Fox after Ray expressed his concerns.

"Tell me about it," bemoaned Ray. "I don't want to stop, though."

"I don't either. Although..." Mister Fox began. "No, that would never work."

"Tell me!" Ray cheered.

"Well, it might be a stupid idea, but... what if I chose the stories instead?"

"You?" It surprised Ray that this had never occurred to him before.

"I'm a very good storyteller, and I've been meaning to practice, but I'm too shy for a real audience. We're friends, though, so I trust you. What do you say, Ray?"

"I say let's do it!"

Mister Fox's stories worked a little differently. Ray could feel a pair of hands, no, they must have been paws, hover mere inches away from the sides of his head. The hairs on the back of Ray's neck stood up from the sensation. The scene around them changed like it usually did, but there was a difference in quality that hit Ray immediately. When he was controlling the story, there were no details in the worlds they entered that Ray did not purposefully put there. Here, though, there were sights and smells and feelings that made the whole thing feel real, more like a memory than make-believe.

They were on the open sea once again, but this was a battleship, not a fragile wooden pirate vessel. Ray could smell the ocean breeze, and he felt the sun beating down on his brow. But he wasn't Ray right now, he was Gordon, a petty officer third class, and he was occupied with helping his crew locate a German U-boat that was supposed to be in the area. It wasn't as dramatic as the pirate adventure had been, but Ray was utterly captivated by the authenticity. Gordon's stress and anticipation were his, and when the crew cheered after one of their torpedoes finally sank the enemy ship, Ray cheered with them. He was truly in the moment in a way he just hadn't been all those other times. When Ray awoke that morning, he was covered in a hot, satisfied sweat.

"It was great!" he told Mister Fox the next night.

"I'm so glad you enjoyed it!" beamed the imaginary friend.

"Can we do another one, like right now?"

"Oh..." For the first time, Mister Fox sounded reluctant.

"What's the matter?"

"Well, you see, I'd love to tell you another one of my stories; I really would. But while you're experiencing the story, for me, I just have to sit here doing nothing. That's hardly fair, is it?"

"I guess not."

"Well, what if... yeah! What if you tell me a story while I tell you one?"

"Would that even work?" Ray questioned.

"Yeah!" said Mister Fox. "You wouldn't even have to do anything; I could just look at some of your boring old memories. Would you let me?"

"Why would you want to look at my memories?"

"It's just something to keep me occupied, that's all. What do you say?"

"I suppose that's okay," Ray relented. "What do we have to do?"

"Repeat after me," Mister Fox explained, placing his invisible paws on either side of Ray's head as he had done before. "I am you, and you are me. We are together, individually."

Ray did as he was told, repeating the words without stuttering or making unnecessary pauses. The scene changed immediately. This time, Gordon was drinking in a bar. Ray had never been inside a bar before, but he had seen Homer Simpson visit one on TV loads of times, which had often made him curious what a real bar was like.

Gordon was drinking beer. Ray could taste it, and he thought it should have been yucky, but to Gordon it was nice and refreshing. It made Ray feel like a grownup, a sensation more intoxicating than the beer itself. He took another sip. When he put the bottle down, a pretty lady was staring at him from across the bar, and that made Ray feel very grown up. He didn't know why, but it was strange, and his face got hot. Why did Ray want to go over and talk to her? He didn't know that either, but he was thankful that Gordon started to get up.

They didn't make it far before a man neither Ray nor Gordon knew staggered up to them and pushed Gordon aggressively. He spoke with a slurred speech, and his center of gravity seemed to be off. The man blabbered something about Gordon making lovey eyes at his girl, half his words impossible to make out from the drunken stupor he was in. Without warning, he punched Gordon directly in his nose, and it hurt bad enough to make Ray want to cry.

"It's only a memory," whispered the voice of Mister Fox in Ray's ear. "The pain only feels as bad as you let it."

While Ray tried not to feel the hurt so completely, the scene continued. A second punch from the drunk man failed to connect. Gordon took this opportunity to catch his fist, and delivered his own blow by pulling the man in closer. Already having trouble staying upright before the fight, the man went down right away. From the floor, he made an awkward lunge for Gordon's legs, but Gordon retaliated by kicking him in the head. When he fell back onto his side, Gordon kicked him again, and again, and then a fourth time.

The violence was scary for Ray, but just like the pain he'd experienced before, he tried to keep himself from feeling that fear, and it worked. Instead, Ray felt triumphant, like he was a big, strong man who couldn't be pushed around. It was something he wanted more of in his waking life, so here in his Imagination Room, he cherished the encounter, even if hurting another person made him a little uneasy.

Ray never saw that pretty lady again, but Mister Fox had more stories with other pretty ladies in them. Sometimes they just talked with Gordon, something Ray had little experience in with the girls at his school, but other times there was kissing, which Ray had decidedly no experience in. Before now, Ray hadn't even known that was something he wanted, something that he now sorely felt the lack of. And sometimes, there were stories with far more than kissing in them, things Ray had no concept of, but made him feel funny all over; excited and ashamed, proud and tired, happy and queasy, all in equal measure. Ray liked it, and he was all too happy to trade Mister Fox memories of his boring life, memories of bike riding or sitting in class or having family dinners, for more.

Mister Fox didn't always give Ray stories like that, but they were usually just as exciting. Gordon wasn't a soldier forever, but he still used a gun sometimes. He ran with a gang that reminded Ray of him and his own friends a little. They would make fun of each other sometimes, but it was all in good fun, and they ultimately had each other's backs. Sometimes they'd need to shake down people who owed them money. Ray was amazed when Gordon shoved a gun in someone's face, a boy not even ten years older than Ray himself.

"Do you believe in God? Are you afraid to die?" Gordon asked without ever raising his voice. The boy responded by wetting his pants.

"Nothing like the movies," Ray sighed in astonishment after he woke up back in his room.

The time Ray spent with Mister Fox began to have an odd effect on him. There would be mornings he woke up and felt like he had not slept at all, hardly less tired than he had been the evening before. This lack of energy made it hard to focus in school, but even in rare instances where he wasn't exhausted, he could not get Gordon's adventures out of his head. Memories of ordinary dreams tended to fade a few hours after waking up, but these stayed with Ray like he had actually lived them. As a way of coping, he had begun recording them for creative writing assignments, which made him popular with the student body but a menace in the eyes of his teachers.

"You didn't get in trouble, did you?"

"A little," Ray admitted one night. "They said I have an inventive voice and should keep writing, but the subject matter wasn't appropriate for school. I had to write an apology to my teacher, but that was it."

"Aww, what do they know?" laughed Mister Fox. "Besides, that's not what you really want to tell me about, is it?"

"No," Ray said happily. "All the kids in my class, at least all the boys but some of the girls too, thought your stories were so cool! Everyone wants me to hang out with them at recess. And I'm going trick-or-treating in a few days with the coolest kids in class!"

"Is Halloween so soon?!" Mister Fox babbled. "I had no idea. But that's wonderful, Ray. I knew people would appreciate you as much as I do, once they got to know ya."

"I really love all the stories you've been telling me," Ray admitted.

"And *I* really love getting to live in your memories!" When Mister Fox got excited like this, it felt to Ray as if one ear heard him like he was shouting from far away, and the other heard him like he was whispering right up next to it. "It's an amazing thing being an eleven-year-old boy."

"What?" laughed Ray. "It's okay, I guess."

"You've got it all wrong," sang Mister Fox. "You're healthy, and you've got your whole life ahead of you. You got out of trouble at school because you're a child, so people gave you the benefit of the doubt. Imagine what else you could get away with. Not to mention you're from an economically stable family, which ensures a good future! You have limitless potential, Ray Brady."

"I think I wanna talk about something else..."

"Of course, of course. I'm sorry, Ray; I got carried away. How would you like to experience what it's like to be in a real live car chase?"

"Wow, that would be amazing!"

"You know what to do," said Mister Fox.

"I am you, and you are me. We are together, individually."

This time, Gordon was in the driver's seat of a car. Ray couldn't wait to be old enough to start driving, so being behind the wheel with Gordon's confidence was like a dream within a dream come true. One of Gordon's friends sat in the passenger seat, hanging out the window while firing a gun at another car that was tailing them.

"You can't aim for shit!" Gordon yelled at him. The back of Ray's neck felt hot from the illicit thrill of cursing.

"You think you can do better, hotshot?" shouted his friend.

"As a matter of fact, I do! Take the wheel, chowderhead!"

The chowderhead leaned over into the driver's seat while Gordon grabbed his own gun from off the floor. Ray was too anxious to aim properly, but Gordon knew exactly what to do. It only took him three shots before the other car did a hard swerve into a stop sign, a column of white smoke erupting from under the crumpled hood.

"You crazy bastard!" said Gordon's friend. "Alright, credit where credit is due, you saved our bacon."

"Hey!" Gordon scolded. "Look alive, we're not out of the woods y—"

A police car appeared out of nowhere and rammed them from the side, sending the car into a spin that would put some roller coasters to shame. Gordon didn't see them coming, so Ray didn't either. Mister Fox had taught him how to shut out the bad feelings, but the collision was so sudden that Ray felt like he might be sick. His eyes blinked open, but he wasn't in his bed.

"What are you doing awake, Ray?"

"Mister Fox...?"

Ray was sitting on the floor in his family's living room just a few inches away from their TV, which was on but only playing static. His whole body was numb, like the pins and needles feeling that comes when your leg falls asleep, but all over. His eyes were stuck on the screen, where Ray could just barely see his own reflection staring back at him. His face was warped slightly, elongated, and his eyes looked bigger and yellower than he remembered. Were his teeth larger as well? He tried to lean in for a closer look, but the pins and needles kept him paralyzed.

"Did you not like the story, Ray?"

"Why am I out of bed, Mister Fox?"

"Oh." Mister Fox rarely hesitated when he spoke, so it set Ray on edge to experience it now. Was Ray's mouth moving with his words? "You just had so many good memories watching television, I wanted to give it a try."

"But nothing's on."

"I'm an imaginary friend, Ray; I've never watched television before. I thought I should practice first."

"Can I go back to bed now? It's late and I'm tired." More hesitation from Fox, more unease from Ray. After a few seconds, the TV switched off without anyone touching the knob or a remote, and feeling returned to Ray's extremities.

"Sure thing," said Mister Fox in his usual happy voice. "Sweet dreams, friend."

The next morning did not go Ray's way at all. This was just the latest in a series of mornings where he had woken up feeling cranky and irritable, actual rest apparently being hard to come by, with or without strange conversations with his imaginary friend in the middle of the night. To make matters worse, this was the morning his mother delivered some of the worst news Ray had ever gotten.

"What do you mean I can't go trick-or-treating?!" he whined.

"I'm sorry, sweetheart," Mrs. Brady said sympathetically. "Your dad's business trip got extended by a couple days, and I got called in for a shift at the hospital, so there's no one to take you."

"I can go by myself!"

"Yeah, no way," said Ray's mom, trying to sound cool.

"But Mom, all my friends are going!"

"Well maybe they can share their candy with you at school next week."

"Mom, no one shares their candy."

"Really?" gasped Mrs. Brady. "That's so cruel. But fine, then I guess, if you're good, we can go out and buy some cheap candy on November 1st."

"It's not the same, Mom. All my friends are expecting me to go! This is so unfair!"

"I said no, Raymond. You're only eleven years old, and the streets are dangerous at night. You can stay home and watch Halloween specials. Charlie Brown will probably be on, and I saw a commercial yesterday for *The Halloween Tree*. You loved that book!"

"Screw you, Mom!" Ray shouted, putting more hate and vitriol into those three words to his mother than he had ever used in their entire relationship. He'd never come so close to cursing at her before, but he'd learned that and a lot more from Gordon, who he was certain wouldn't stand for this if their roles were reversed.

Mrs. Brady's face went through a whole spectrum of emotions. First was wide-eyed shock, then hurt, then incensed rage. But all those gave way to a disturbing sort of calm which made Ray instinctively pull back from his mother. She didn't strike him; that was something she would never do. Instead, she pulled a box off the top of the fridge and made sure

Ray saw the label: an assortment of little chocolate bars which were all her son's favorites.

"Your father and I got these for you to give out to trick-or-treaters," Ray's mother said emotionlessly. "And we would have conveniently looked the other way if you just so happened to take half the box for yourself." Without another word, she strode across the kitchen, tossed the box in the garbage bin under the sink, and tied the bag for disposal.

"I'm going to put this in the garbage can outside. When I get back, you better be in your room, and I don't want to see you until dinner." Ray did as he was threatened, slamming the door to his room loud enough that his mother could hear it outside.

"Mothers can be so cruel, can't they?"

"It's not fair!" Ray sobbed into his pillow. "I could totally go by myself! This is so stupid, it's—" His tantrum was suddenly undermined by the realization that something was not as it should be. "Mister Fox?"

"Yes?"

"It's daytime."

"Yes."

"And I'm awake."

"What's your point, Raymond?"

"I only ever see you at night when I'm asleep."

"It's nearly Halloween," chuckled Mister Fox. "The veil between worlds is thinning. Life and death, time and space, imagination and reality; all sorts of things are possible this week!"

"Wow," Ray exclaimed earnestly, his woes briefly forgotten. "That's so cool! Halloween is... oh."

"Oh, don't cry, Raymond." Ray thought he could actually feel a hand land on his shoulder, although the grip was a little too tight to be comforting.

"It's not fair," he repeated. "Kids don't get to do anything. If I was bigger, they'd let me go."

"Would being Gordon make you feel better?"

"Y-Yes," Ray sniffed.

"Alright," said Mister Fox. "Lie back; I can talk to you while you're awake, but you need to be sleeping for this part."

"Okay."

"You know what to say, Raymond."

"I am you, and you are me. We are together, individually."

Ray was out immediately. Every other time Ray had dreamt about being Gordon, it had felt incredibly real, not like a dream at all. This time was different, though. Scenes came to him in flashes. First it was immediately after the car crash from the last adventure. Gordon's forehead had been split open when it hit the steering wheel, and his associate, the one Ray only knew as 'chowderhead,' had smashed his head on the passenger-side window. He wasn't moving. A police officer was approaching the car and shouting something, but Ray couldn't make it out.

Next, they were in a courtroom. The judge was also shouting at Gordon, but Gordon wasn't listening. He was angry and spiteful, screaming inside. The courtroom shifted to a jail cell, four concrete walls and a bed that was just a small slab that jutted out from the wall. Ray didn't like this place, so he tried to force the scene to change again. But he couldn't; it was just this room, again and again, those same four concrete walls day after day and night after night. The only way Ray knew time had passed was because Gordon had taken to scratching tally marks on the wall. His right index finger was perpetually bloody, since he had nothing else to make the marks with, and you could follow them by how the wall was stained more and more red.

Ray's consciousness flailed like he was drowning, desperately treading water to keep from going under. He wanted to get out, and he was still kicking and screaming before he realized he was back in the Imagination Room. White mist and black static surrounded him. A few feet away, if one could even measure distance that way in a place like this, he saw his own body, but something was horribly wrong.

It looked as if his body had been deflated like a cheap balloon, and a long gash had been drawn up the side. No blood or guts spilled out, though. There was just empty space. A creature was hunched over the body. It was the color of rust, its own form stretched horribly, with long limbs and a curved, boney torso. Ray couldn't tell if it was covered in flesh or fur, but it looked incredibly moist. More horrifying than its appearance, though, was the fact that it seemed to be trying to crawl inside Ray's body.

"Stop it!" was all Ray could shout in protest, fear running over him like a cluster of spiders.

The creature spun around to snarl at Ray, its inhuman lips pulling back to reveal sharp, needle-like teeth. Its entire face was an uneven mixture of human and animal characteristics, but Ray couldn't help but focus on its familiar yellow eyes, which were big and emanating rage in his direction. When the creature lunged forward and hissed, Ray yelped and fell backwards.

Suddenly the Imagination Room was gone, and Ray was lying back in bed. But it wasn't his bed, and it wasn't in his room. A musty smell choked the air, a fragrance lying somewhere between an antique store and a public washroom in the middle of summer. It was incredibly dark, despite it having been day time when Ray had gone down. He tried to get up, but his body ached and had no energy. After an exhausting effort of craning his neck to look around, Ray saw slits of light escaping the sides of blackout curtains, confirming that little time had passed.

Everything hurt when he lifted his hand, but he fought to make his feeble eyes adjust to what little light there was. The hand Ray saw was not his own, but a frail, wrinkled appendage that looked and felt like it might break in two with minimal effort. Then he saw the index finger, which was whittled down and scarred at the tip, and Ray screamed for a long time.

Nobody heard him.

The thing inhabiting the body of Ray Brady had a busy forty-eight hours leading up to Halloween. He made a point of apologizing to Ray's parents for the boy's earlier outburst. Mrs. Brady said she accepted the apology, but it did not change the fact that Ray was still not permitted to go trick-or-treating, and even if it did, she had already returned his costume to the store. Ray's body said that was okay, neglecting to mention he was already wearing a better disguise.

Ray's friends didn't notice any change in his demeanor, but that was to be expected. Though some had not yet fully grasped how to be kind human beings, they were all innocents, ignorant to the dangers that the world could offer up. None of them were on the alert for predators, let alone ones within their own social circle. To them, Ray was the same as he ever was, and his recent exploits in writing were still fresh in their minds. When 'Ray' talked, they listened.

"It's a real haunted house," said the body of Ray Brady. "We can visit it while we're out getting candy."

"I dunno..." said one of Ray's friends uneasily. "Haunted houses are creepy."

"What's the matter, chicken?"

There are few who are more susceptible to poultry-based insults than an eleven-year-old boy among his peers. It was such a simple bit of name-calling, one which didn't actually mean anything, but the results spoke for themselves. The boy who had raised the objection, who the thing inside Ray's body hadn't bothered to learn the name of, had ousted himself as a potential weak link in their group, and none of the others wanted such heat to fall on them. Therefore, rather than agree with a fairly reasonable protest, they kept their mouths shut and went along with group consensus to see a haunted house.

Home alone with no supervision, the body of Ray Brady made its egress from the house and began a long walk across Whisper Falls. It may have been too tiring of a trip for the real Ray Brady, but the interloper in his skin was driven by dark purpose, and had enough wisdom to pace himself so as not to expend all his energy. The parents of a few early trick-or-treaters shot him concerned glances as he passed them by, but chose to mind their own business and said nothing. There were an excessive number of teenagers out, but they were too busy being embroiled in an escalating prank war to be of any concern to the solitary traveler.

When the group of boys finally assembled, they engaged in some rudimentary trick-or-treating on the way to their destination. The creature masquerading as Ray Brady relished every minute of it. It had been decades since he had properly enjoyed candy, but he had aims to develop a taste for it once again. Ray Brady's body had young, healthy blood, and a strong pancreas which could contend with the richest sugars.

The house that 'Ray' had told them about was located on Moundshroud Crescent, a poor neighborhood even for the poor part of town they now found themselves in. The buildings there were mostly low-income apartments and other houses over fifty years old that were not regularly maintained by their owners or the city. As they encountered fewer homes with porch lights lit and decorations on the front lawn, urban code for 'no free candy here, buzz off,' the mood of the group changed. Not a single boy there could honestly say he wasn't scared by the prospect of a real haunted house, and the thing inside Ray Brady had really sold the authenticity, but some were better at hiding it than others.

They instead voiced concerns that trespassing on private property might result in being punished, so the group swore itself to secrecy about what they were up to tonight. No matter who asked them and regardless of what went down, they would not speak of it. 'Ray' of course joined in; after all, he had no reason to share what he was about to do with anyone after the deed was done. Perhaps a lover, someday, since he planned on having several, and the usual pillow talk was bound to get dull eventually.

The thing pretending to be Ray Brady laid out the rules for their little game. One by one they would go inside, steal some object of significance, and come back out, not revealing what they stole until the very end. When all was said and done, they would compare their treasures, and whoever had the best thing would be the winner. Ground floor was in bounds, but the upstairs was strictly off-limits.

"Why?" asked one boy dressed as a pirate.

"Why?" laughed the entity that was not Ray Brady. "That's where all the murders happened, so the haunting is most concentrated on the second floor. None of us would survive up there. They'd find a bunch of mangled bodies with their faces forced into bloody smiles if we tried."

A collective gulp could be heard from the rest of the group. The most insecure boys volunteered to go first, and 'Ray' let them. It didn't matter, really. The murder backstory was entirely fictional, and the rules of the game were completely made-up, just a convenient ruse to facilitate bringing a bunch of patsies along should things go sideways. The first few to return reported a definite haunted feeling when they were inside, and strange noises coming from upstairs. When it was time for the presumed Brady boy to enter the house, he did so with confidence and gusto.

Mildew-infused air filled his nostrils. It was a scent he was painfully familiar with, and one he'd be happy to never smell again after tonight. There were no lights on, but he could navigate with no issue. The same apparently could not be said for Ray's companions, as there were end tables and dead, potted plants that had been clumsily knocked over. None of that impeded the body of Ray Brady from making its way to the stairs.

There wasn't much to the second floor, just a short hallway with a couple of rooms on either side and a dingy bathroom right at the top of the stairs. The bedroom at the end of the hall was his destination. He didn't bother avoiding the spots in the floor that he knew would creak; what lived in this house wouldn't be able to stop him whether it heard him coming or not.

He entered the room with no fanfare. It was especially dark, blackout curtains keeping out what little illumination the streetlights outside projected. There was some light within the room, though. Tall machines stood on either side of a small bed, blinking dozens of little lights and making the occasional beep.

And in the bed lay a shriveled, corpse-like man who was staring at this new visitor.

“Muh...muh...” moaned the corpse. It spoke as if it hadn't had a glass of water in months.

“Can hardly speak under your own power. Pathetic.”

“Muh... Mister Fox...” said the man in bed with great difficulty. “Is that... you? Why do you look like me? I... I don't want to play this game anymore.”

“You seem to be operating under two delusions, friend,” said the thing that was not Ray Brady. “For starters, I’m not Mister Fox; I’m Ray Brady. You are Gordon Fox, veteran, who only ever enlisted because your own father said you were a worthless worm who couldn’t make something of yourself otherwise. Gordon Fox, who was so angry at the world after the war ended, you jumped at the first chance to turn that anger outward when the mob was looking for recruits.

“Gordon Fox,” he said, pushing his face incredibly close to the man’s, feeling the old body’s stale breath even as he went on with his diatribe, “who wouldn’t sell out his fellow mobsters to the police, but whose fellow mobsters didn’t show him the same courtesy. You’re Gordon Fox, the man who wasted a majority of his life in prison, and who only got older and sicker and more pathetic after you got out.

"The second delusion you're suffering from is that we're playing a game, because the game is already over. You lost; no point in being a sore loser about it now."

"I want to go home," whined the true Ray Brady, but the thief who had stolen his body wasn't finished speaking.

"You're not special, you know." The body of Ray Brady pulled back, grabbing a pack of cigarettes and a zippo lighter off an end table. He lit a cigarette, regarded it for a minute, and then stomped it out, deciding it was best not to spoil his new vessel already. "I'd been bedridden for so long, body spent, but my thoughts as sharp as ever! I was a prisoner once more. I got good at calling out into the void with my warped and twisted mind. You were just the first rube to pick up the phone. Well, congratulations, you got everything you wanted—you're a grownup now."

"Mister Fox... everything hurts..."

"I told you my name is Ray Brady!" To send his point home, he actually struck the old man square in the face. Ray Brady's body may have lacked strength, but the body of Gordon Fox lacked constitution, and so got a bloody nose even from the feeble punch. Ray Brady whimpered in pain. He would have started crying, if Gordon Fox's tear ducts weren't so ancient and impotent.

"If I can say one comforting thing to you, though," continued the usurper, "it's that you won't be in pain for much longer." He placed his hand on a plug which fed into the two life-support machines that flanked the bed. "Goodbye, Gordon Fox." And then he pulled the plug.

The devices made one angry, drawn-out beep before turning off completely. Their lights would never inadequately illuminate this room ever again. Things were silent after that, but the sound of Ray's worsening breath gradually intensified.

"Why... are you doing this?" he asked Mister Fox, someone he had at one point considered a close friend and confidant.

"I was wondering that myself." The body of Ray Brady spun around sharply, now on alert with the presence of a third voice in the room. The body of Gordon Fox couldn't move nearly as fast, but was equally alarmed.

"Who are you?" demanded the soul of Gordon Fox. "You aren't one of the brats I came here with."

"You know me," said the little boy. His face was pale, with dark bags under faded cyan eyes. He wore a charcoal gray fall jacket with a matching newsboy hat. In his hand was a blue balloon on a string.

"Ah, you're right— I do recognize you. I've caught glimpses of you before, several just this past year. Look alive, worm," he called back to the man in the bed. "Ha! You're in the presence of Thanatos, also known as Joe Black. The Grim Reaper, Death himself, and I think he's here for you."

"Why are you doing this, Gordon?" Death asked.

"Why?!" he repeated. "Why else? I'm not ready to die! My life was a colossal waste, but I'm wiser now. I was dealt a bad hand, so I deserve a second chance. I earned it, me! I claim this body as my prize. Its previous occupant was undeserving, and in it I will achieve wonders."

"Is that all?"

"Yes, that's all. And before you ask, yes, I'm proud of myself too."

"Give the body back, Gordon."

"Excuse me?"

"I said give the body back."

"You must be joking."

"Everything has its time, and everything dies. Even I'll die, someday, when the Universe no longer needs me. If you're as wise as you claim to be, you'd recognize that. So, I'm asking you to give the body back; don't rob this boy of his go around because you're unhappy with the choices you made during yours."

"Feh!" shouted Gordon Fox. "You can stand there and judge me all you like, but I don't have to listen to you anymore! Do you know why? Because when this body eventually wizens and falls to ruin, I'll do the same trick again. I've outgrown you, Reaper. The insight of age and the endless advantages of youth, savored across hundreds of lifetimes. I'm practically a god now, and I will do as I like."

Death narrowed his eyes. "I'd be mindful of what night it is when calling yourself a god, Gordon Fox. I have never been quick to anger, but there are other deities out tonight who are more easily offended than I."

"Chatter away all you like," scoffed the body of Ray Brady. "I have places to be— it's Halloween, and I'm a small boy. There's candy to eat, houses to cover in toilet paper, merriment and mayhem to be had! This is a house of the dead, and I'm bound for the living!"

Gordon Fox ran out of the room without looking back once. He made his way down the stairs and escaped through the backdoor. His unwitting companions out front may have heard him, had their attention not been drawn elsewhere by the sound of explosions and mortified screams off in the distance. Death watched him go, disappointed but not surprised, before turning back to Ray Brady.

"You're... not really a kid like me, are you?" Ray asked.

"I'm not."

"That makes sense. You're... you feel like a grownup."

"You're very astute, Raymond Brady."

"Everything hurts, mister," wheezed Ray.

"Let me help you with that." The little boy approached, and suddenly Ray felt very afraid.

"Stop!" he shouted. "Don't come any closer. I... I want my mom and dad."

"They're not here, Raymond. I'm sorry, but I'll do what I can for you." When Ray made no further protests, Death placed a hand on his shoulder. True to his word, it did help, and the body Ray was trapped in no longer hurt. The pain was replaced with a kind of empty feeling, one which made Ray sad, but was still preferable to the sensation of his organs shutting down one by one.

"That's... a little better."

"What happens next is going to be a little scary," said Death. "But I promise you that it isn't all bad. Look at my balloon, Raymond."

Death lowered the balloon so it floated just a few inches away from Ray's head, and the boy did as he was told. Despite the darkness of the room, the orb still possessed a reflective sheen, and in it, Ray saw three dead grandparents, his family dog Molly, who had tragically passed away two years ago, and half a dozen goldfish, none of whom had lived past six months, but Ray had loved all equally.

"You won't be alone when you go," Death promised. "And it won't ever hurt, never again. Now, I want you to take a deep breath and hold onto this balloon for me."

Ray reached for the string, but hesitated at the last second.

"What's wrong, Raymond?"

"It's just... I can't stop thinking about Mister Fox. It... isn't fair. He cheated! And now he's probably going to hurt a lot of other people."

"I wouldn't worry about that," Death said warmly. "I'm not the only god of Halloween working tonight. It's true, Gordon Fox was a cheater, and the sad reality of life is that sometimes cheaters win. But they also never prosper." Ray nodded, understanding in his heart if not in his mind, and took the balloon.

Three blocks away, another god was stirring. The Violent Dark, lord of fear and patron saint of fiends, killers, and madmen, was whispering in the ear of Kevin Salt, and all it took was two words. The calling inside Kevin Salt did not originate from the Violent Dark. That corruption was a demon all his own, so it was not the deity's place to instruct, only inspire. The two words were "Moundshroud Crescent," and they sent the killer on his path.

He was accustomed to moving in shadows, taking indirect routes and ducking into back alleys and side streets on the way to his destination, though he never made it that far. In a small path that cut between two neighborhoods, Kevin Salt spotted a solitary young boy, the only one he had seen tonight without a Halloween costume. The boy walked without a care in the world, and so didn't notice he was being followed. By the time he could sense the danger he was in, it was too late. Gordon Fox fought back, but despite the endless advantages of youth, there was no contending with the strength of a grown man with evil intent in his heart.

The body of Gordon Fox was discovered on the morning of November 2nd, when a court-appointed nurse named Morgan Alex made her weekly visit to the residence. She reported to police that despite the condition of the body, it appeared to be smiling. The body of Ray Brady was never found.

They never found out what happened to Ray Brady.

Vermilion Moon

"For a witch stands on the very edge of everything, between the light and the dark, between life and death." -Terry Pratchett, The Shepherd's Crown

The town of Whisper Falls only had two bars that were over fifty years old. Any other pubs or taverns that could have made a similar claim had all closed over the past couple decades due to a combination of bad reputations and economic turmoil, and the two that remained just so happened to fall on opposite sides of the city map. On the rougher side of town was Stingy Jack's, a dive which credited its longevity to its namesake, as neither Heaven nor Hell seemed to want to claim it. On a crisp autumn day late into October, an emaciated man in a golden jacket sat alone in a corner booth.

"Can I get you anything while you wait for your friend, hun?" asked a cocktail waitress.

"He's not my friend," grumbled the man, almost to himself.

"Okay, well can I—?"

"Say," the man said as if he were noticing the waitress for the first time. "I'llwageryoutwoyearsoflifethatyou'llgetmyorderwrongjustsaywhatifyouagree." He said the entire sentence in a single breath with no pauses.

"I'm sorry, what?" said the waitress. "I didn't catch that."

"Never you mind, dear," said the man in a slower cadence, failing to completely hide a sinister smile. "I'll have a pinched lager, and do be quick about it."

The waitress left in a huff, offended enough to not realize that she didn't know what a 'pinched' drink was. The man in the gold jacket could have explained that it was a regional slang, although not this region, that had not been used in over half a century to refer to drinks served with a slice of pear, but that would have ruined the grift, and he wasn't prepared to let that happen.

"You look absolutely dreadful," said a short, rotund man who had just approached the booth.

"Edwin!" the man in the gold jacket greeted before needing to cough just from the light exertion. "I was starting to think you weren't coming."

"I wasn't," said Edwin Murd. "But it's been a slow day at the shop, and in spite of myself, you've piqued my curiosity, so I'm having the Gaunt boy man the till."

"How's that pathetic cripple doing?"

"Still pathetic and crippled, but he has his uses." Edwin Murd sat down opposite the man. "He's only so dependable, though, so I won't be out long. You have ten minutes, Gamesman. Make it good."

The waitress returned and set one lager down in front of the Gamesman, no pear in sight.

"Oh, that's just lovely!" he cheered, invigorated by the years won from his ignorant opponent.

"Anything for you, sir?" she said to Murd before putting a hand to her forehead and staggering slightly.

"No, but I'm sure I have something for you, Olivia Selick."

"How do you know my name?"

“I’m very good at reading prospective clients,” was the only explanation Murd offered. He produced a glossy business card with dark lettering and handed it to her. “Do visit my shop if you find yourself in want of something... more, out of life.”

“Right...” Olivia backed away slowly before bumping into another table, startling her. “J-Just holler if you need anything, I guess.”

“Feeling better, then?” Murd asked disdainfully.

“It’s a temporary remedy,” groaned the Gamesman. “I’m not strong enough for a bigger ante, so I have to subsist on scraps.”

“I was sure you’d have expired by now,” Murd chuckled. “I’ve been waiting to collect your coat for my shop. That Willows brat really did you in. Happy Halloween, by the way.”

“We’re still more than a week out!” The few scattered bar patrons turned in annoyance towards the Gamesman before returning to their drinks and conversations. “I’m sick of temporary remedies. What I need is a cure! This is what I’ve called you here to discuss, Edwin. I propose a wager.”

“I got tired of your wagers a long time ago.”

“You know what I’m about. You wouldn’t have come here if you weren’t at least willing to consider the idea.”

“Touché.” Murd crossed his arms and leaned back in the booth.

“My proposal is this,” said the Gamesman, waving his hand for showmanship. “A bet for your precious immortality.”

Murd snorted. “Your sickness has made you even more stupid than usual, which is a feat.”

“You’ve gone on at length in the past about what a curse living for so long has been!”

“Yes, but that doesn’t mean I’m in any sort of hurry to destroy myself, especially in a way that benefits you.”

“Oh, don’t be so dramatic.” The Gamesman took his first sip of the lager and immediately spit it out. “Tastes like piss.”

“I assume you wouldn’t put forward such an audacious motion if you didn’t have something of your own to offer up?”

“My jacket,” he said with no hesitation.

“Ha, not good enough.”

“You just said how you’ve been waiting to add it to your shop!” whined the Gamesman. “Here’s your chance.”

“It is tempting,” Murd admitted. “But I could also just wait for you to expire from your own ineptitude and risk nothing.”

“I’ve acquired a lot of knowledge over the years, Murd.” The dying man leaned partway over the table, his tall shoulders and yellow eyes making him resemble a bird of prey. “For this, I’d bet the jacket and every dark piece of lore I have rattling around inside my skull.”

"...what precisely are we betting on?" Murd asked after a moment's consideration.

"As I'm sure you know, it's a vermilion moon tonight; a full moon equidistant from Friday the 13th and Halloween."

"You don't have to define it for me, you gibbering cad."

"It's the first vermilion moon in almost a century, and you know what that means."

"Curtis Walker..." said Murd, who began to put together where this conversation was going.

"This backwater, hick burg hung that bastard for what he did to them."

"He wanted to be mayor." Murd recited the fact like he was reading it from a textbook. "When he lost the election, he made sure the constituents knew how he felt about it."

"And swore he'd return on the next vermilion moon to exact his vengeance. To this day, people still don't know whether to classify him as a serial killer or domestic terrorist."

The pair sighed as if they were schoolboys lauding the exploits of a superhero or star athlete.

"What exactly is the wager, Gamesman?"

"Simple, I bet you that Curtis Walker will return as he promised and wreak havoc on Whisper Falls. By Halloween the town will be in ruin, whether that be physically or emotionally. This rotten place chewed me up and spit me out; it would do my rotten heart good to be saved by its destruction."

Edwin Murd contemplated the Gamesman's words. It was true, he had lived a long and miserable life. He had consorted with kings, traded arcane secrets with other wicked shopkeepers and peddlers and snake oil salesmen. He had garnered a reputation, inadvertently, of being a man lacking a certain level of intelligence, at least when compared to those mages and madmen who deal in magic. But he was cleverer than most would give him credit for, and that was how he liked it. He also had a flair for the dramatic, and an insidious creativity that rarely allowed him to take an interesting idea at face value.

"I admire the degree of spite that went into this," he said, steepling his fingers theatrically. "But it feels rather... boring."

"You're not serious," scoffed the Gamesman. "I'm talking about the vindictive soul of a maniac tied to a once-in-a-century cosmic event returning to cause untold carnage on a quaint little community! What more could you possibly want?"

"It just so happens I did make one sale today. My store was visited by four snot-nosed brats just after lunchtime who were looking for cheap entertainment. I normally shoo away such riffraff with extreme prejudice, but then I recalled how much is possible on a vermilion moon. Primordial magic literally fills the air. So, I may have given them a map... to the hidden grave of Fairuza Gulch."

"I'm not familiar with that one," the Gamesman said indifferently. "Old girlfriend of yours, Murd?"

"She was a powerful witch, at least according to local legend. This town destroyed her much like they would Curtis Walker years later. She had children, who had to renounce her in order to avoid suffering the same fate, but they petitioned the townspeople for the right to bury their mother's body deep in the woods. One of them drew a map so they could find it again, which over the years eventually made its way to my shop."

"Of course it did."

"I sold it to those children, who wanted to see something 'totally insane.' I also scrawled some rudimentary resurrection phrases on the back of the map. Nothing too potent in the hands of children any other day, but today? Well, season of the witch and all that."

"I think I see what you're getting at, you living ventriloquist dummy." The Gamesman took another sip and spit it out. "We're betting on horses, figuratively speaking. You, the witch, and me, the prodigal son."

"First one to destroy Whisper Falls wins?"

"We should draw up specific terms..." the Gamesman put forward.

"I'd expect nothing less from you," Murd smiled, equally jubilant, conniving, and hateful. "Are you sure your constitution can handle this one?"

"Oh, please. For a permanent solution to my woes? It will be a piece of cake." The Gamesman took one final sip of his drink, this time managing to swallow it. "This Halloween is sure to be one this town won't forget."

One day short of a week later, four children were desperately combing through the Whisper Falls Public Library like their lives depended on it. This was a difficult undertaking, seeing as only one of them had ever set foot inside a real library before. Rhonda Dougherty had often found refuge in here when the weight of the world around her was too much to bear. She was learning that being the 'weird girl' wasn't such a solitary fate, and that outcasts could be found in all walks of life, but that didn't make it any easier when she went misunderstood or unappreciated.

She felt responsible for the predicament they were in, even though it had been a unanimous decision to go into that weird store, and they had all pooled their pocket change to buy the map to Fairuza Gulch's burial site. But she had been so excited to go, to pay her respects to a real witch. And, when her curiosity had gotten the better of her, she read the funny words on the back of the map that she was now certain had brought Fairuza back.

Only Cole knew, and that was because it had come out during a panic attack the following day. He was too good of a friend to hold it against her, and the twins would have been too, but she was anxious about more people finding out, even if they were her only other friends. Because didn't this prove she might be a witch too, like she had suspected for so long? There was so much conflicting information out there, though, and it wasn't like Whisper Falls was crawling with witches she could ask for clarification or guidance.

"None of this makes any sense," said Cole, startling her back to reality and echoing her own thoughts. "I've read at least four books about witches, and they all seem to contradict one another. Some say anyone can learn to be a witch, others say it's something you're born with. One book says only women can be witches, but another implies there are boy witches too. I read one that describes casting spells like it's just whatever the witch wants to happen, but a lot of others say you need the right words and ingredients and symbols to do it."

"I think they're all sort of right?" said Rhonda, before being hit with a wave of uncertainty. "Or maybe none of them are, I don't know." She put her face in her hands and groaned in frustration.

"Hey, we're not beaten yet." Cole tried to sound encouraging, but he had his own doubts that he was grappling with.

"Halloween is in three days," Rhonda said, hands still over her face.

"Maybe the twins found something?"

"We did!" called a voice that immediately earned them a shushing from Ms. Nightshade, the head librarian.

Leslie and Nathan Mancuso were something of a sideshow in Whisper Falls. Though different genders, they looked uncannily alike, since neither one wished to cut their hair short. Leslie tried to combat this by wearing hers in a ponytail, but their similar height, eye color, and jawline made it impossible to not draw comparisons. If that weren't enough, they were scarily good at knowing what the other one was thinking or feeling, at least most of the time. One of the first instances of this had been when the pair was six, and Nathan could tell that Leslie had gotten her foot caught in a sinkhole while she was out exploring the woods. She had been missing for hours, and once they found her, their mother called them both the Wonder Twins from then on. They definitely shared some kind of spark, which was what had drawn Rhonda to them in the first place; she had a knack for discerning when someone was 'special.'

"Where have you guys been?" asked Rhonda, finally emerging from her finger cocoon.

"Reading!" Leslie and Nathan each had a stack of books in their hands, and a quick scan of the titles on their spines told Cole that the twins may not have understood the assignment they were on.

"Leslie..." he said with concern. "What do you have there?"

"Oh, let's see. *Wizard of Oz*, *The Witches* by Roald Dahl, *The Chronicles of Narnia*, *Macbeth*. They've all got witches in them."

"I'm not sure they'll have anything useful," said Rhonda. "But points for creativity, I guess. Nathan, what have you got?"

"I'll be honest," he began sheepishly, "I may have just grabbed some books off the return cart and gotten distracted. I've learned a lot about our town, though! Like, did you know Whisper Falls is actually on top of a fault line? Or that until twenty years ago, the mayor could pardon *any* crime if it was perpetrated within city limits? Or that there's a rare plant that only grows here and a few other places in the country that—"

"Nate, this is serious!" Rhonda objected, cringing a bit when she got a stern look from Ms. Nightshade. Quieter, she said, "Fairuza has been loose for a week and could be—"

"Hold on," said Cole. "Nathan, let me see that one there." From the bottom of his stack, Cole pulled a book entitled *A Comprehensive Guide to Witchcraft* by Morgan Alex. "This one wasn't on the shelves where I found the others. Nathan, you're a genius."

Nathan made an exaggerated show of looking flattered. The four each took a seat around the table while Rhonda flipped through the book. Cole thought it read pretty similar to the other books he had seen today. It provided clarity on some of the contradictions that had vexed him, but it introduced a whole new host of discrepancies that made his head hurt. There were diagrams in this one, though; things like pentagrams and other less recognizable symbols, types of familiars and sacred sites like stone circles. There was one drawing, however, which made all four of them recoil back from the table like a firework had just been dropped there.

"You know I like you kids just fine," said Ms. Nightshade, who had come over with a pained look on her face. "But if you can't cool it today, you'll have to go; I don't make the rules. Actually, I do, so I'm not afraid to enforce them."

“Understood,” said Rhonda, whose gaze was glued to the floor.

“So, we all agree that was what we saw last week?” Cole asked once the librarian was out of earshot.

“Yeah,” said Nathan, grabbing the book. “I’d never forget a face like that.”

Rhonda pulled the book back to get a better look at the image. It was a woodcut-style illustration depicting a forest of tall, thin trees, and just right of center stood a humanoid creature, partially hidden behind the trunk of a tree. Its body was horribly thin and bent at uncomfortable-looking angles. It wore no clothes, and was covered in dozens of small cuts and bruises, some of which looked like they formed symbols. It reached out a single gnarled hand, the index finger twice as long as it should be, and its fingernails over six inches long. Its mouth, which only had about six crooked teeth inside, hung open in a way that could neither be described as ‘happy’ nor ‘sad’; ‘predatory’ was the only word that fit. Long, black, stringy hair hung down over the top half of the creature’s face, but hateful, burning eyes could still be seen peering out from within.

“‘The Beldame,’” Rhonda read aloud. “‘Black magic is not inherently the same thing as witchcraft, but one can often be a path to the other. The witch who relies too heavily on black magic, either by becoming dependent on necromancy, being consumed by negative emotions, or consorting too flagrantly with the dark powers, may corrupt their flesh to the point that they lose their humanity. A beldame is a parasitic creature, spreading pestilence and feeding off the lifeforce of local wildlife and any nearby populace (favorably children) to fuel a trail of sadistic pandemonium.'"

"A lot of kids have been absent from school this week..." shuddered Leslie.

"And my mom says none of the grocery stores have had fresh produce lately," added Cole.

"Not to mention the obvious one," said Rhonda. "Pumpkins have been rotting all over town. A Halloween without jack-o'-lanterns would be bad enough even without all the other stuff."

"Great," Nathan said sarcastically. "The book confirmed what we already knew. Now can it tell us how to kill her?"

"Whoa," exclaimed Cole. "Who says we're going to do anything besides tell an adult? We should call the police, or maybe the army."

"We're the ones who woke her up," Leslie argued, her lip quivering. She genuinely believed it was the right thing to do, but, as she was starting to learn, that wasn't always the safe or preferable thing.

"Yeah..." squeaked Rhonda, a fresh pang of guilt catching in her throat as she tried not to think about how the blame should be divided. "Getting anyone else involved would just be putting them in danger, and that's if they even believe us. We've all seen dozens of movies where adults never believe kids when there's a monster running around. We can do this ourselves."

"How?" the rest of the table said in unison.

"The book says we can use holy water," Rhonda explained. "Silver, too. Purified salt, certain herbs. Iron, if it's used in certain ways."

"Silver and holy water?" Nathan scoffed. "Is this a 'bel-dame' or a demon werewolf? Oh, I wonder if it's too late to change my costume for this year..."

"Focus, brother," teased Leslie. "Rhonda, you know the most about this stuff; what do you think we should do?"

Rhonda scanned the pages on the beldame several times. "I'm going to make a list."

The group reconvened after a late lunch, eager to get their tasks done quickly. They still had more than half the weekend left, but some of the things they needed might have been trickier to find than others, and then they actually needed to execute their half-baked plan. School on Monday would severely limit their maneuverability, and Tuesday was the 31st. None of them could say for certain why Halloween felt like the precise deadline they were working under, just that it seemed like if they didn't stop Fairuza by then, something *bad* would happen.

Their Saturday afternoon was spent running around town raiding gardens, churches, grocery stores, a pioneer village, and even their own homes for things they hoped could hurt a beldame, if one book by an author none of them had ever heard of could be trusted. They paid for what they could, which wasn't a lot of it, and took the rest with silent self-admonishment and a promise to behave better when lives weren't at stake.

There was no shortage of old churches in Whisper Falls, so they each took turns visiting different ones, usually filling up a bottle with holy water when no one was looking, but Nathan had just asked a priest directly and was given some with no suspicion or fuss. Their collective haul was emptied into two large jugs and mixed with salt, herbs that Leslie ground up with a rock, iron shavings from the pioneer village smithy, and a heaping of makeup, whose primary ingredient was silver powder, that Cole had 'borrowed' from his mother. They poured their concoction into four water guns purchased from Montani's Toys, on sale due to being summer items this late in autumn. The sheer absurdity of what they were doing made them all cringe a little, but they felt empowered too, like they were comic book characters or the heroes of their favorite after-school specials.

There were signs of something amiss in Whisper Falls all over. As they had gone about their errands, they had seen smashed windows, dead plants, power surges, and a pet store where every animal had apparently become hostile at the same time early in the morning. Leslie volunteered to interview as many people as she could (her honest nature had prevented her from participating in too much of the theft, however well-intentioned) and had gotten a timeline for when most of these phenomena occurred. Cole made marks on a map of the town and saw a relatively straight path of strife.

Now it was simply a matter of putting themselves on that path.

They made hasty excuses to their parents that they had been invited to each other's houses to do homework and were subsequently asked to stay for dinner, ensuring they would have at least an hour after dark to find the beldame and make quick work of her. And if it took them longer than that? Then they could say they lost track of time, or that biking home took a little longer in the dark. After spending the last of their allowances on burgers and chicken nuggets, they rode towards where they expected Fairuza to be.

"It's quiet," Rhonda observed, scanning the strip mall for signs of trouble. A man behind the counter of a convenience store glared at them warily through the front windows.

"Too quiet," chuckled Nathan. "I've always wanted to say that."

"With everything that's been going on," said Cole, "people probably don't want to be out at night, even this early."

"Uh, guys?" chimed Leslie. They followed her eyeline to a small building next door. In a window on the second floor, a light was flickering wildly.

It was a power station of some kind. The whole property was surrounded by a chain-link fence, but the padlock on the front gate had been broken and thrown to the ground. A gray sedan was idling out front over three parking spaces, with one wheel up on the curb.

“The witch has its driver’s license?” said Nathan.

“Could be one of the beldame’s victims,” Cole guessed.

“Oh,” Leslie moaned. “Maybe we shouldn’t be here. Cole was right, we can tell the police.”

“We’re going inside,” Rhonda declared. “Once we find her, I’ll put this iron horseshoe we got from the pioneer village in the doorframe. The book said she won’t be able to cross it that way. Just to be safe, I’ll pour a ring of salt around us too. Once we’re protected, we blast her with the anti-beldame spray.”

Everyone nodded their uncertain approval before heading inside. Every door or gate they encountered had been opened, some simply unlocked but others looked like they had been forced. There were safety signs everywhere, warning them about the dangers of proceeding without hardhats and proper protective equipment, something that made them all uneasy. They carried on up a flight of stairs and down a hallway, at the end of which flickered the light that led them here.

“Alright, guys. This is it,” said Rhonda. The group pumped their water guns in preparation, and Rhonda tossed the horseshoe into the doorframe from a safe distance. She regretted the ‘clang’ it made when it landed, and the flickering stopped. “Go!” Rhonda wailed.

She didn’t even look in the room, focusing on making sure the salt ring was unbroken. The rest saw inside, a room filled with large, humming machines that had dials and switches. Standing inside was a single figure, a pale, middle-aged man wearing dark blue coveralls. He stared at them blankly, and though they all wanted to pretend they hadn't seen it, his eyes had a subtle green glow.

"Now!" Rhonda roared after completing the circle. They sprayed him mercilessly, and his disgusted reaction made them believe their plan was working. After twenty seconds of constant dousing, they lost water pressure and had to pump again. During this time, the man approached the door and looked down at the horseshoe.

"The witch probably shapeshifted to blend in," Rhonda wheezed, exhausted by the effort it took to charge her gun. "But it can't cross the door. We're almost there!"

And then the man stepped out of the room towards them.

"No!" shouted Leslie.

"T-The salt will protect us," Rhonda stuttered. "Get ready to fire again!"

Still wearing a blank expression, the man lunged across the barrier and picked up Nathan by the throat with one hand, the boy's water gun crashing to the floor.

"Nathan!" his sister cried. Cole attempted to grab their attacker, not really sure what his plan was beyond that, but the man gave him a hard shove in the chest that knocked him down and sent him sliding across the floor into a wall.

"Well, this is interesting," said the man as he squeezed Nathan's neck. "You brats think I'm that creature that's been terrorizing the town?"

"Y-You're not?" Rhonda replied.

"Let go of my brother!" screamed Leslie.

"This body's name is Alan Gaunt," said the man, "but my name is Curtis Walker. I don't suppose you've heard of me?" The group, minus Nathan, shook their heads.

"Typical; Whisper Falls never did know how to educate its youth. Alright, you precocious ragamuffins. I'm on a tight schedule, so we'll skip the formalities and cut right to the chase. Ghosts are real, the afterlife is real, and so is *Hell*!"

Curtis emphasized the last word by making his eyes glow more intensely, and the kids screamed.

"And a long time ago, your stupid and deceitful forefathers sent me there. So now I have one chance —this century, anyway— to make this town pay. Thanks to the technical knowhow and weak mental fortitude of Alan, here, I have the perfect way to make that happen."

"The power surges," Cole groaned as he struggled to get up off the floor. "That's your doing, whatever you're planning."

"Poor Alan hasn't been okay for years, so worn down by grief and regret for what happened to his family. He's hardly fighting back in here, his heart's that spent. But that will just make it easier for me to overload the Whisper Falls power grid. Look at me, using terms like 'power grid'; I've become so modern already!"

"You can't do that!" Rhonda shouted.

"Our infrastructure would collapse," said Cole. "Hospitals would be helpless. Food couldn't be refrigerated."

"Hospitals, grocery stores," Curtis echoed with maniacal glee. "No traffic lights, or telecommunication devices. The cells at the prison up on the hill would all unlock at once. Not to mention all the fires and explosions that would happen in such a short span of time. It's really too perfect. This Halloween is sure to be one Whisper Falls won't forget."

"Not if—" Nathan coughed. "Not if I kick your ass first."

"Oh, you're not making it out of tonight alive," said Curtis. The emotion in his voice had been fluctuating until now, but he said that completely deadpan, like it was a fact and not an idle threat, and that terrified them more than if he had been howling and snarling. When he started to walk away, still choking Nathan, they were too paralyzed to react.

"Stop!" Leslie shrieked when Curtis was halfway down the stairs.

"I've caused a fair bit of other mischief, you know," said the ghost as Rhonda, Cole, and Leslie gave chase. "The power grid needs to be undermined gradually, that way no busy-bodies notice until it's too late. So along the way I've smashed a few windows, thrown a few pets in the creek when no one was looking. But I think Whisper Falls is wicked and worthless and rotten enough that it deserves something special. A dead kid in town square would be just grand, don't you agree?!"

Leslie and Cole threw themselves at the body of Alan Gaunt as it walked outside with Nathan, who was starting to go blue in the face. Neither of them was particularly big or strong for their age, though, and Rhonda was still too stunned to do anything more than follow.

When they reached the front gate, Curtis froze the way a deer does when it hears a twig snap in the forest. Something was off, and eventually the kids sensed it too.

"You stupid brats!" he shouted before dropping Nathan. "The streets are deserted. Four unescorted children are like a beacon for the beast!"

This brought Rhonda to her senses. She followed Curtis's vision to a streetlight that flickered at the far edge of the parking lot. Now that she was focusing on it, she could see a crooked figure standing just beyond the glow. It took a cogent step forward, then another, and then the horrible thing they had woken up deep in the woods was less than twenty feet away from them. Leslie began to cry and covered her eyes as she reached a hand out where she thought her brother was. Nathan wheezed, the color slowly returning to his face. Curtis let out an inhuman wail from his stolen mouth before leaping into the driver's seat of the sedan. He left so fast that the tires made skid marks on the road.

Rhonda, meanwhile, stood transfixed. Whatever quirks she possessed that had made her suspect throughout her life that she may be a witch, they were working in overdrive this week. She could tell when things were going to happen before they happened, not world-changing occurrences but little things that nevertheless couldn't be ignored. Her empathy was higher, people's moods being easier to read than a newspaper. Even her dreams were more vivid, too complex to completely interpret, but giving her enough of a lead to aim her and her friends in the right direction when it came to their mission. It was as if there was something in the air supercharging all that was uncanny in her, and that something was connecting her to Fairuza now.

She could feel her body in the parking lot, but Rhonda's other senses were in the beldame's mind. She saw so much, like the witch had twice as many feelings in place of thoughts, and all of them were angry. None of it was sequential, starting with a firsthand experience of her barbaric execution, followed by a scene of Fairuza in prison while her children renounced her. Pain, betrayal. She spent so long in the ground, rotting, being absorbed by the roots and the earth, turning the roots and the earth black with her hate, waiting. So much waiting. The image that lasted the longest was the waterfall that gave Whisper Falls its name, which began to flood with rain, drowning everything around it before the water turned to blood.

Cole was the first one to notice that Rhonda's eyes had turned white. Though it pained him to look directly at the beldame, when he put together what was happening, he didn't hesitate to spray it with the only remaining water gun. The beldame's skin hissed, but the witch herself let out a pained noise that didn't sound like any natural being on Earth. It was enough to sever the connection with Rhonda, who fell to her knees and vomited up her hamburger. She could still feel remnants of Fairuza in her mind, but when she looked back to the streetlight, the witch was gone.

Cole helped Rhonda to her feet, and Leslie helped her brother. They rode their bikes home in silence, nobody sure what to say. On the way, a raindrop hit Rhonda on the head, a seemingly insignificant event that portended something awful...

It was still raining by Sunday morning. Even if the four weren't haunted by what they had experienced last night, the incessant tapping of raindrops on their windows would have ensured they woke up unrested and groggy. The weatherman confirmed that this torrential downpour had literally appeared out of nowhere, turning what should have just been a mildly overcast week into a wet and gray mess.

"It's the beldame," Cole said during their three-way phone call. "It has to be."

"It is," Rhonda added grimly. "I saw it, when our thoughts touched. It looked like she was going to flood the town."

"As if rain on Halloween wasn't bad enough," Leslie muttered.

“Not...” Nathan said before coughing. His strangulation by Curtis Walker had left his throat red, and his vocal cords strained and raspy. “Not a flood,” was all he could get out before coughing again.

“Nathan,” tutted Leslie. The Wonder Twins had to both use a single phone and struggled to be heard equally. “Save your voice. If you write down what you want to say, I can—”

“Take too long,” he wheezed. “I can do, talk slow. I read it in... library, the fault line beneath town. It said on the news that the sewers are too old... can’t handle so much rain at once. But won’t flood.”

“What are you getting at, Nathan?” Rhonda asked.

“Ralph Dyniaski.” Cough, cough. “He told me at school about how the sewers aren’t just old. Lots of weird tunnels, some go on forever and ever. That much water... pouring into the earth...”

“It could cause an earthquake,” said Cole, his fear petrifying him so completely that he actually sounded calm.

“Right on Halloween night, I’m guessing,” surmised Rhonda.

“If Curtis Walker’s power surge doesn’t get us all first.” There was anger in Leslie’s voice now, almost venom.

“Doomed,” Nathan said sombrely. Though he lacked the strength to express the sentiment more complexly, they all understood what he meant: one way or another, they were royally screwed. None of them knew what more they could say.

"Not long now," chirped the Gamesman.

"It's all over, as they say, but the crying." Murd was absent-mindedly tidying his shop, as whether he won or lost their bet, he'd likely need to make a swift egress from Whisper Falls. It wouldn't be the first time he left somewhere in a hurry when things turned sour. Although, if he'd known that the wager would involve so many frequent visits from his opponent in his place of business, he might not have made it, spoils be damned.

"What's this thing do?" the Gamesman asked, picking up a chalice made from deep green glass with a lattice pattern on its surface.

"Put that down!" scolded Murd. "That cup is ninety percent of all the Oznium on this planet; I won't have you getting your currish fingerprints all over it."

"Fine," he pouted. The Gamesman returned the cup to its place on the shelf and surveyed the domain of Edwin Murd with fresh perspective. "Maybe after I've won your immortality, I'll take up ownership of this place."

Murd made a face like he had just bitten into a rotten egg. "I think if it came to that, I would welcome oblivion."

"Are you worried at all about the children?"

"Do you have a specific set of children in mind, or are you broadly referring to the youth of today?"

"The brats you had wake up the witch."

"I haven't given those cretins any thought since we made our deal."

"Well," the Gamesman said impishly, "they're sticking their noses in where they don't belong. They had an encounter with Curtis and Fairuza, both in one night."

"Oh," said Murd. He had paused his tidying when it seemed like the Gamesman might actually have a valid point to make, but when he was convinced that this wasn't the case, he got back to it.

"Is that all you have to say? What if they taint our wager?"

"These urchins are bees sensing an intruder in their hive. They might land a few stings, but they fail to realize that the intruder is not a wasp, but a bear; they no more have the power to stop it than they do to snatch the sun from the sky."

The Gamesman narrowed his eyes skeptically. "You're really so confident?"

"I don't need to be." Murd stared out his storefront window, watching the rain hammer the glass mercilessly. "I'm sure, those children won't know what to do until it's too late."

"I know what to do," Leslie told the group during their next phone call after suppertime. They would have met earlier in person, but the anxiety brought about by the weather made their parents wary about letting them leave the house.

"We're listening," Cole assured her.

"Okay, so," Leslie began. Her and Nathan didn't have a lot in common apart from looks, but occasionally their personalities aligned, and they had all heard Nathan begin many long-winded stories and unhinged rants that way. "What we have are two equally apocalyptic threats hellbent on destroying our way of life and ruining our Halloween, right?"

"Right," said Rhonda.

"Well, what if they just canceled each other out?"

Rhonda waited for someone to say something. When no one did, she asked, "what do you mean, Leslie?"

"Curtis said Fairuza found us that night because we're kids, and no one else was around, so she was able to hone in on us. Our young energy, or whatever. And Curtis was afraid of her. So, what if... we just lure her to Curtis and let them fight each other?"

"Whoa," Cole sighed after another pause.

"Yeah," Leslie continued. "He's an evil ghost, so he'll probably be able to hold his own for a bit at least. And if Fairuza beats him, we can just hit her with our anti-beldame spray, and before you know it, she's melting like the witch in *The Wizard of Oz*."

"What made you think of this?" asked Rhonda.

"I'm tired of being so afraid all the time." Leslie's voice was shaky, like she was on the verge of crying. "And I love Halloween, and this stupid town we live in. I want both to still exist in November."

"She's right," said Cole.

"But mainly, Curtis Walker hurt my brother. One way or another, he's gotta go down." She still sounded upset, but Leslie's voice wasn't shaking anymore.

"I..." Rhonda murmured.

"Let's do it," Cole said decisively. "Leslie's right, I'm tired of being afraid. And how many comic books or movies have we seen where someone has to fight evil when no one else can or will?"

"No." Rhonda clasped a hand over her mouth as soon as the word slipped out.

"No?" Leslie repeated indignantly.

"They'll..." Rhonda started before poking a head outside her bedroom door to make sure her mother wasn't within earshot. "They'll kill us!" she hissed once she was confident that they could speak freely.

"They'll kill everyone if nobody stops them," Cole inferred.

"Someone else will. We can't do this." Rhonda couldn't believe what she was saying. In her heart, everything Leslie said had resonated with her, and a part of her recognized that her friend had never sounded cooler than she did a minute ago when she was making her case. But her heart was also heavy with fear and doubt, which had taken executive control over her mouth.

"Wow," Leslie scoffed.

"Rhonda, we can do this," said Cole, trying to sound reassuring.

"What does Nathan have to say? We should put it to a vote."

There was a minute where no one spoke, but Cole and Rhonda could hear whispers and muttering from their respective phones.

"He..." said Leslie. "He shook his head and walked out of the room."

"So that's a tie, then." Rhonda thought she sounded pathetic and desperate, but didn't know how to change that. "That means we don't do it."

"That's not what a tie means!" snapped Leslie.

They argued after that, for longer than any of them would have liked. By the time the last of them had angrily hung up their phones, not one of them could have said they were particularly looking forward to Halloween this year...

School was canceled on Monday. Fairuza's rain continued to fall, and road conditions had only worsened since the weekend, meaning no yellow buses would be taking to the streets. Both of Rhonda's parents had left for work by the time the call had come in, leaving Rhonda all alone. She hadn't slept well, so it only took an hour or two at home for her to become edgy and unsettled.

The world was ending, but she was thirteen, so this was far from the first time she had felt that way. Unable to stomach watching game shows and old sitcoms any longer, she opted to do what she always did when things felt hopeless: go to the library.

Clad in a black raincoat with matching boots and a bright yellow sou'wester, she trudged her way through the deluge. The weather report hadn't been lying; some streets were entirely submerged in water. There was wind, but it had no effect on the raindrops, which pelted Rhonda mercilessly at a ninety-degree angle.

The library was open, but no librarians greeted her when she got there.

"Ms. Nightshade is the only one who came in today, so she's busy doing work in the back."

"Nathan? What are you doing here? How's your throat?"

"Better," he winced, rubbing the faded bruise around his neck. "Honey tea has helped a lot."

"Is your sister with you?" Rhonda asked warily.

"No, her and Cole are getting ready to... you know."

"Yeah... so why are you here?"

"I didn't want to die with overdue library books."

"What?" Rhonda laughed, caught off guard by the fact that she was still capable of doing so amidst all her troubles.

"The world is ending, right?" Nathan smirked. "I'm... what do they call it, getting my affairs in order?"

"You're ridiculous." Rhonda shook her head, but smiled as she did so.

"And now I guess I'm just hiding from the rain."

"Can I join you? I don't think I want to be alone right now."

"Sure," said Nathan. "Come on, I made a fort out of books in the corner."

They passed the time reading. Neither one held onto one book for very long before moving onto another, Rhonda because of her anxiety and Nathan because of undiagnosed ADHD. When she couldn't focus, Rhonda found herself staring at a large map of Whisper Falls that hung on the wall.

"Do you really think it's all just going to be gone tomorrow?" she asked Nathan.

"I don't know. I feel like they've been saying the end of days is coming since our parents were our age."

"Probably a lot longer," Rhonda conceded.

"Yeah, I guess since Bible times, maybe?" They both shrugged. "But the world is still here, despite everything. There's gotta be something to that, right? Maybe things just work out, one way or the other."

"Nathan..." Rhonda hesitated. "This is all my fault."

"What?"

"When we visited Fairuza's grave, I read some magic words on the back of that map. I don't know for sure, but..."

"The evidence is pretty conclusive, huh?"

Rhonda put her hands over her face, wishing desperately that she could just withdraw into herself and disappear. What pulled her out was a comforting hand on her shoulder.

"That guy who gave us the map was a friggin' creep." A powerful belly laugh shot out of Rhonda, and she had to fight to keep quiet. If Ms. Nightshade heard them, she didn't care enough on a day like today to scold them for it.

"Thank you for that," Rhonda said gratefully. "After everything that's been going on, I haven't been laughing much lately."

"My point being," Nathan went on, "is that it's hardly your fault. The map just so happened to have the right words to wake up a beldame? I smell a set-up."

Rhonda had never thought about it that way, and she felt like she could cry from the relief it brought her. Instead, she said, "I want to help your sister and Cole, but... what can we do?"

"You're a witch, right?"

"Yes?" She wasn't used to someone being so blunt about that. Most people who knew how she identified tended to either condescend to her about it or shy away from the subject entirely.

"Then why don't you just cast a spell?"

"I don't think it works that way."

"Sure it does. Remember all those books we read? A bunch of them said all a witch needs to do to cast a spell is want it and believe it's possible. So cast a spell that can tell us how to save the day."

Rhonda grappled with these ideas, but given that they were on a deadline, she knew she couldn't grapple long. She had learned about meditation in this very library, so she called on what she remembered and closed her eyes, cleared her mind, and focused on her breathing. So many emotions swirled inside her head, but she fought to hold them back, not wanting to taint whatever spell she was casting. Intention was key, so she focused on the library itself. This was a house of knowledge, haunted by the ideas of the authors whose works lay within and the trees who made the paper they were printed on.

"Please," she whispered, begging the Universe for salvation. "Give me the knowledge I seek."

Her eyes shot open and were involuntarily pointed towards the town map. Lightning flashed outside as time slowed down, casting eerie light inside the library. Dozens of spiders began to crawl over the depiction of Whisper Falls, their shadows thick and vibrating. They sunk their fangs into the town, injecting dark splotches along the surface of the paper. A single fly came along and was caught up in their webs, made to dance against its will like a puppet on their strings. The spiders receded, and more flies came. When they saw what had been done to the map, they tore apart the first fly without a second thought.

Rhonda wanted to scream, but she held a hand over her mouth, somehow aware that if she let the scream out, her revelation would go with it. Time resumed its usual flow, and she shot backwards as if returning to her body after being somewhere else.

“Ow!” she shrieked when her head banged into a shelf.

“Whoa,” said Nathan, helping to steady her. “That was freaky. Your eyes went white and you wouldn’t answer me.”

“They did? I wouldn’t?” Rhonda couldn’t help but smile, but before she could take pride in her first real spell, thunder crashed outside and she felt it inside her skull. “I… I know what to do!”

“You do?” Nathan asked in disbelief.

“Yeah, but we need to make a stop first. Come on.”

The streets of Whisper Falls had largely been deserted. Flooded roads and high winds gave many the excuse they craved to tell their bosses that they weren’t coming into work today. Town square lay empty, save for two children and two foul creatures of the night, the latter of whom were locked in combat. Cole and Leslie struggled to stay on their feet, feeling like the rain itself was trying to push them to the ground. They had both independently concluded that their water guns would be useless in this weather, leaving them hoping that the fight between Fairuza Gulch and Curtis Walker would be evenly matched.

Sadly, the beldame far outclassed the vengeful spirit. No matter what Curtis hit her with, usually a trashcan or sometimes a whole car lobbed with psychokinetic finesse, Fairuza would not go down. To make matters worse, the body of Alan Gaunt looked sickly and pale, his skin practically hanging off the muscle, which gave Curtis little to work with.

"So this was a bust," Leslie said, having to shout over the wind even though her friend was just inches from her.

"I think I felt the ground shake," said Cole. "Fairuza's plan, it's happening."

"I guess that's the end, then." Leslie stopped fighting gravity and let the storm push her down.

"Not yet it's not!" cried Rhonda.

"Oh my god, Nathan!" Leslie wailed, pulling herself back to her feet and wrapping her arms around her brother.

"The world-class witch of Whisper Falls has a plan," he announced happily.

"What are you holding?" Cole asked Rhonda.

"A big stick!" she replied with a smile.

Rhonda and Cole were both thirteen, an age where there's a certain societal expectation that children will start to put childish things away and begin looking ahead towards adulthood. But they were still children, and so remembered those unwritten and unspoken laws of childhood that just about every kid knows, things like the authority that being the first to call dibs on something brings, or how a parent counting to three is one of the most compelling forces in the cosmos.

Or how a cool stick you find on the ground is never *just* a stick.

“I need to talk to them,” Rhonda explained. “And I don’t think they’ll listen unless I meet them on their level, so we stopped by the park. This stick... no, this staff, it’ll give me the boost I need, I just know it.” She pushed past her friends towards the dueling monsters.

“Wait!” said Cole, grabbing her wrist. “You can’t just go up to them, they’ll kill you!”

“They’ll kill us all anyway if no one stops them.” Rhonda didn’t dare turn around; she knew that even in this rain, her friends could tell that she was crying. “I’m sorry for being stubborn before.”

“Rhonda...” Leslie whimpered.

“Hey!” Wind roared around them, so Rhonda really had to howl if she had any hope of being heard. But if either of them could hear her, it wasn’t enough to make them cease trying to destroy each other. Curtis had fallen at the witch’s feet, and Rhonda could feel animalistic hate radiating from the pair. If she didn’t do this right now, all would be lost.

“FAIRUZA GULCH AND CURTIS WALKER!” For a split second, it seemed like every bit of rain and wind had stopped, creating a deafening silence, and the two fiends looked directly at Rhonda. “I have something to say to you both, so you’re going to listen to me!”

Then the storm hit her anew, and she nearly lost her balance. Her yellow rain hat shot off her head and went bounding down King Street. Rhonda watched it go, then immediately cursed her lack of focus, for the two monsters started moving in her direction with frightening speed.

She gulped, but tried to take an intimidating stance. "You're going to listen, do you hear me?" She took her staff and slammed it into the ground the way she imagined Gandalf doing so when she read *Lord of the Rings*. "You will listen! You've got to listen! You, oh—"

Cole saved her from falling, holding her free hand. Leslie had his other hand, and Nathan held her remaining hand in both of his. This time Rhonda let herself look back, and she saw her three closest friends in the world, who were scared and tired and drenched, but more than all of that, they were there for her, and she had everything she needed.

She faced Curtis and Fairuza again, taking a deep breath and clearing her mind. She set her intention clearly in her thoughts and beseeched whatever forces were at work in Whisper Falls for help in completing her task. The last remnants of the vermilion moon responded, giving her the power to change the world in ways she never would have believed. When she spoke again, she didn't need to scream.

"Listen," said Rhonda Dougherty, practically whispering. When she tapped her staff on the ground again, the world faded away into a silent, empty void, black yet bright at the same time. She was alone with Fairuza and Curtis, although she could still feel her friends, their individual sparks lighting the fire in her.

"What is this?" said Curtis, looking around like a desperate animal in a cage. Fairuza said nothing. Even now, Rhonda couldn't stand to look at her for more than a few seconds.

"I can't let you destroy this town."

"Well, that's not really up to you, is it?" Curtis mocked. "And why shouldn't I? This town destroyed me, so it's only fair."

"That may be true," said Rhonda, doing everything she could to keep her voice even. "But there's something you don't know."

"What's that? That you're going to 'kick our asses' like your little friend so confidently claimed the other night?"

"I'm not here to fight you. I'm here to tell you the truth, which is that you shouldn't be fighting each other! You're... you're family!"

"You have got to be joking," said Curtis, although not until after a lengthy pause.

"My 'little friend' helped me figure it out, actually. He learned that the mayor of Whisper Falls used to be able to pardon any crime committed within town limits. That's why you wanted to be mayor, isn't it?"

"I..." Curtis hesitated. "My revenge is all I've thought about for so long. I forgot... yes, I wanted to be mayor. It was all I cared about in the world."

"Why?"

"A family member, a distant one..."

"A grandmother, perhaps?"

"Yes! My great-great-grandmother. She was wrongfully convicted. Everyone in my family knew that story. When I lost the election... I was so angry! I got drunk and attacked somebody, one of my opponents. I was so ashamed, so I ran away into the woods. When I came back, the town turned on me and said I murdered so many people."

"The new mayor used you as a scapegoat to get a few of his buddies off the hook, and in exchange they became his financial backers. Your legacy is a lie, Curtis— a ghost story that got out of hand."

"This was all for nothing?"

"Not nothing." Rhonda took his hand and put it in Fairuza's, although touching the beldame was cold and uncomfortable. "Fairuza, I know you're hurting. What your family did... they were just scared, trying to survive. But they never turned their back on you. They loved you!"

The pale and shriveled thing that had once been Fairuza Gulch staggered back, but Curtis held onto her.

"Is it really you?" he asked, his malice replaced with reluctant hope. The witch never spoke, but she did raise her disturbingly long arms above her head. Rhonda and Curtis both braced themselves for some curse or hex, but what they got instead was something they couldn't have anticipated. Fairuza Gulch, alleged witch and confirmed beldame, a loveless thing that should have had no warmth anywhere in her twisted form, embraced her grandson in a hug.

Rhonda took a step back on instinct, as waves of energy began to emanate off the pair. A light sprang up from where the gap between their two forms had been, and Rhonda had to shield her eyes as both their bodies contorted and curled into one another. There was a flash, and Rhonda fell backward.

She blinked. When she opened her eyes again, she was back in town square. The wind and the rain had stopped, and the storm clouds were parting at blazing speed. An ancient but healthy oak tree had appeared in the middle of the road where Fairuza and Curtis had been standing, soaking up fresh sunshine. The body of Alan Gaunt lay at the base, emaciated but alive, and muttering something about chess.

Rhonda looked to her friends. They had all been standing, but one by one they got down on the ground and held her. Some of them cried, some of them remained silent. Eventually, they all laughed, partly from unfathomable relief, but mainly out of an innocent kind of joy. Despite it all, tomorrow was Halloween, and anything was possible.

The next morning, the Gamesman pounded on the door of Curious Oddities.

"Murd!" he cried. "Murd, get out here, you pulp horror cliché!"

"Hmm?" said the shopkeeper, finally arriving at the door after making sure to keep his unwanted caller waiting. "Oh, Gamesman, I'm surprised to see you; I was sure you'd be looking for a gutter to die in somewhere by now."

"Save it. Our wager was invalid. I demand a do-over."

"It wasn't invalid, there were just unforeseen variables."

"I literally foresaw those children being a problem!"

"Even so, a draw is a draw, Gamesman. Take it, and maybe you'll die with at least a shred of dignity."

"I refuse!"

"Perhaps a shred was a generous estimate..."

Suddenly the Gamesman doubled over, his sickness making the inside of his skull throb mercilessly. When his eyes had ceased watering, he noticed a figure down the street watching them, a little boy in a gray coat holding a blue balloon.

"No!" he shouted at the boy. "You stay away from me! It isn't my time yet, do you hear?"

Murd glanced in the vague direction that the Gamesman was accosting. "Who are you talking to?"

"I'm sick of Halloween," he spat, his gaze fixed on Murd but his arms out and swaying as if he were addressing an audience. "A night dedicated to ghosts and goblins; it's pathetic. Recently I've been aimless, but now I think it's my duty to remind this world of something."

“And what’s that?” Murd asked dispassionately.

“That monsters aren’t relegated to one night of the year! They’re out there, in the shadows. I might be dying, but dying isn’t dead, and a wounded animal is the underestimated monster. You think I’m finished? I’m just getting started!”

Murd watched the madman careen down the street with all the grace of a drunken honey badger, only returning to his shop when the Gamesman took a sharp left onto Main Street and disappeared from view. Prior to the interruption, he had been hanging a sign in his shop window which read, ‘Trick-or-Treaters will be defenestrated.’

“Halloween,” he remarked to himself as he resumed his work. “Always brings out the crazies.”

Afterword

The year was 2020. The world was still relatively fresh into a global lockdown, one which forced us all to stay inside and reckon with ourselves a little. Around early September, after overcoming certain events more traumatizing than anything found within the pages of this book, whimsy began to return to my heart. With plenty of free time on my hands, I got a notion to write a story for Halloween, a special story, which would revolve around one particular character of mine.

Edwin Murd is one of the oldest characters in my canon. An argument could be made that he predates my canon. I first developed him in high school, starting with a repugnant and ugly name that suited his demeanor. A misanthropic and wicked shopkeeper who spends his bitter and lonely immortality pawning off cursed and enchanted objects on unsuspecting customers, he's certainly derivative of Leland Gaunt from Stephen King's *Needful Things*, a book I'd neither read nor heard of when I first came up with Murd, plus countless other similar characters. I owe that serendipity to the horrifying power of pop culture osmosis, as well as the compelling nature of tropes.

By 2020, I'd realized where Murd had come from, so as a way of saying "alright, I get it," to King and the literary world at large, I named Murd's teenaged companion 'Gaunt' as a cheeky way to acknowledge the connection and close that loop. "Halloween Surprise" got decent feedback from the handful of people I convinced to read it, especially my most important fan and critic: myself. It made me want to do the same thing again next year, so I looked to a pair of characters that came to be around the same time Murd did. The Gonzo Brothers, my tribute to showmen and the gothic circus/carnival aesthetic, turned my single holiday tale into a yearly tradition, which led to the book you now hold in your hands.

I poured my heart and soul into these stories. While they differ in content, all of them can draw their origins back to the Halloween-related media I consumed in my youth, the collective feelings they filled me with. While not a conclusive list, the dedication at the beginning of this book names five people I think are responsible for the genesis of *Whisper Falls*.

I love slasher movies. The masked killer is forever fascinating to me, those unstoppable killing machines; monsters with human origins. John Carpenter's *Halloween* did a lot to establish that genre, and it did so by elevating the inherent horror in a holiday I love. And good horror can be born from simple hypotheticals, like "what if the Boogeyman was real?"

And if John Carpenter created the definitive Halloween horror film of the 20th century, Michael Dougherty certainly crafted its 21st century successor in 2007's *Trick 'r Treat.* So much of that film's DNA is in *Whisper Falls.* Halloween having rules, and consequences for breaking them. The power of the holiday as an idea. Even just the basic concept of a collection of interconnected Halloween stories taking place in the same town. And of course, Sam. My gods of Halloween would call him their king.

Speaking of films, I think anyone who grows up watching cable TV has a few films they saw once as a kid, only to never remember the names of and be forced to wonder about for years until Fate gives you the answer by chance. I'd be lying if I said I was a hardcore Goosebumps fan, but I still owe a great deal of inspiration to R.L. Stine for one such movie, *When Good Ghouls Go Bad.* This turn-of-the-century made-for-TV movie is wonderfully weird in the best ways. It fosters an aura that reminds us Halloween can be horrifying, bizarre, and beautiful all at the same time. It's an aura I definitely tried to emulate with *Whisper Falls.*

Another author whose influence can be found all over my interests is Ray Bradbury. The idea for the Gonzo Brothers came directly from the song "The Greatest Show Unearthed" by Creature Feature. At some point I decided to look into the history of the song, and discovered that itself was inspired by Bradbury's *Something Wicked This Way Comes.* After researching the book, I found out it was cited by King and numerous other authors I love as something that influenced their writing. Reading it for myself was thus a delight, and it made me rediscover another one of those forgotten childhood films: *The Halloween Tree*, released fittingly on the year of my birth. If wind could blow through the words on these pages, you'd no doubt hear the wicked laughter of Carapace Clavicle Moundshroud chasing Joe Pipkin's soul across the ages.

And finally, there's Stephen King. Late into the process of preparing this book for publication, likely far later than it should have happened, I looked up examples of King stories set on or around Halloween, realizing it was weird that I couldn't immediately conjure one to mind. It was only then that I learned he quite famously hates Halloween... whoops. I could have simply left him out of the dedication, but deep down in my heart, I knew that was wrong. So, with apologies to Mr. King, but being that you're the undisputed master of horror fiction, I'd say that qualifies you to be an honorary god of Halloween. Thank you for always being a kind and benevolent god.

Special Thanks

That was a pretty long-winded afterword, so if you don't mind, I'd like to cut right to the chase here.

Thank you, Mom and Dad, for always believing in me, supporting me, and doing all that other stuff good parents should do. Even though I don't always act like it, I'm so grateful.

Thank you, Matt, for being my best friend, my brother, and a fellow creative who I can always talk to about the weird world of my writing that exists within my head. I think you're the only person who understands that world on the same level I do (on very rare occasions you may understand it better) and I'll always love you for that, among countless other reasons.

Thank you, Jen Frankel, for being a continuous and consistent mentor, colleague, and friend. My first novel wouldn't have happened as quickly, efficiently, and professionally as it did without you stepping up as publisher, and I owe the same on my first self-published outing here thanks to you being such a spectacular guide. May your kindness and creativity help the whole world someday.

This was my first time employing beta readers, a prospect which was scary at first but ultimately very rewarding overall. A sincere thank you to Emilee, Marcus, and Charlotte for reading my book and giving me your honest opinions and feedback. It helped a lot, and *Whisper Falls* is better for it.

Never judge a book by its cover, yes, but never let your book go without an excellent one. Tina Olah, who I originally contacted about doing one of seven interior illustrations before deciding to go in another direction, took my poorly edited mock-up and turned it into one of the most beautiful book covers I have ever seen. The fact it has my name on it makes me want to cry. My compromise for the interior artwork was to have just one image, the only one I had a clear idea of from the very beginning, and I'm thrilled I got to work with Val Love, who was my first choice to do the cover of *Skeleton Business*, to create it. Edwin Murd never looked so good, and while he may not be big on giving credit where credit is due, I am. Thank you both, from the bottom of my heart.

Penultimately, thank you Kit Daven for a veritable mountain of last-minute formatting assistance.

And finally, thanks to you, dear reader, for picking up this silly Halloween collection of mine. It means more to mean than you can ever know.

About the Author

Steve Bernardi is an author from Ontario, Canada. He loves films, his friends, Halloween, and, perhaps most of all, telling stories. His body of work includes the series *The Bonesbury Chronicles* and *Whisper Falls – the Town That Dreaded Halloween.* He's currently thinking about doing something with bears,* but you didn't hear that from me...

*as in a book. Get your mind out of the gutter.

www.ingramcontent.com/pod-product-compliance
Lightning Source LLC
LaVergne TN
LVHW042112301125
826711LV00005B/20
9781069367402